Love PLUS Loyalty

DeShawn B. Hicks

LOVE PLUS LOYALTY

iUniverse books may be ordered through booksellers or by contacting:

iUniverse
1663 Liberty Drive
Bloomington, IN 47403
www.iuniverse.com
844-349-9409

ISBN: 978-1-6632-2261-9 (sc)
ISBN: 978-1-6632-2262-6 (e)

Print information available on the last page.

iUniverse rev. date: 05/10/2021

L + L = M o n e y

INTRODUCTION

Pary'on walked his 6'1 light caramel complexion, 215 pound frame with atheltic build to his 2017 challenger on 26 inch rims. He sat in the driveway of his nice two level brick side mini mansion on the south side of Miami, Florida rolling a blunt of blue dream sickle, when one of his three phones rang. He looked at the phone screen to see the ID of the caller. And the name stored under 1st lady. He snatched the phone up using his thumb to swipe to answer. "Whats up wifey"? Marie was a very sexy yellow bone with amazing curves. She had a natural K Michelle shape standing 5'3, with long thick hair, with beautiful light brown eyes with pretty ass toes, she never needed a pedicure for. "Turn that music down daddy"! H reached for the knob, as the sounds of Yo Gotti standing in the kitchen decreased. Marie said, "Thank you love". "So what's up baby"? Are you about to pick the kids up? I'm about to now. Marie smiled at how he always on point. "So what do you want to eat tonight? I'm in the mood for some taco salad, taco salad it is". And you have to come get Poncho's prescription. I'll be there as soon as I pick them up". Well ok popi. I guess I'll see you in a lil bit". "Fosho." I love you". I love you more daddy". Impossible, don't make me fuck you up." "Whatever". I'm come fuck you at your job". "Boy you know that cameras are everywhere! Ain't nobody bout to lose their job for your silly ass. Fuck your job girl". "You know daddy got you". Yeah I know. But we are not going back down that road. Hurry up and get the kids so you can bring your sexy ass up here and give me some kisses and let me cop some feels of that dick. "He smiled loving his wifey. She was so sophisticated and lady like, but his super freak on the low. Alright ma'am see you in a minute. "Okay Daddy I kove you". Love you too". Click....Pary'on finish rolling his blunt then fired it up. As he drove, he thought back at how it all began.

CHAPTER 1

I was the summertime of 2006 in South Carolina. And Pary'on had just gotten out of prison doing 3 years non-violent, so he did 18 months all together. He came home to his squad crunching in the streets. Everyone hit him off with either drugs or money or both. It did not take him long to get back where he once was before the prison stint. He stayed up day in & day out hustling. Then one night the city was swarmed by the DEA forcing him to go n the house early. He just sat in his room smoking blunt after blunt bored. He began looking at some of his things he bought home from prison. He stumbled across a site for sexy women. He called it and not long after he set up his profile he met Marie. But Marie lived in Miami. But it was something about her that drawed him to her. So it turned out he was older than her by 5 years. But she insisted she was very mature for him & loved him instantly. She was a real goody two shoe virgin, while he was a seasoned street nigga. And all he knew was the streets. So days went by and he felt as if he could really mold her into his innocent lil perfect wife. But, the streets was who Pary'on really married too. One morning Pary'on woke up to his phone ringing. It was his cousin Al. "Yo" man get your ass up! I've been calling you all morning! "Pary'on pulled his phone off his ear to look at the time on his front screen, 1:23 p.m. His eyes got big as if he was awaken by the smell of the famous Zest soap commerical. "Fuck" Al understanding him. "Yeah nigga! You miss all the money! Pary'on jumped out of bed so fast, he ran to the bathroom to brush his teeth. He ran the shower water, stripping out of his clothes all at once. "I'm up. I'll holla at you in a little bit. "He took a five minute shower. He snatched the towe off the towel rack drying off running to the room to his clothes in a small bag. He got dress in the clothes he bought from the mall the prior day. He snatched his car keys and left out running to his Grand Marquis on 24 inch rims, a donk as they called it in 2006. He raced to the block. As he pulled up in Greenhurst, once he turned on Roberts drive he could look down the road straight to the trap house.

Cars were parked all over the yard in all types of positions. All the main key hustlers were there already. Cars passed Pary'on on his way towards the spot. Cars with waiting customers sat patiently to be served. As Pary'on was pulling his car in the neighbor's driveway due to the packed yard, his homeboy Skeet smiled pointing at him bobbing his head to the Young Jezzy song. I Luv it, as it blared through the two 12 inch subwoofers beating from Pary'on trunk. Pary'on happy to be around his nigga & happy to be back on the block, jumped out dancing a little, hands & head bop rapping the hook with Young Jezzy's new #1 hit record off the inspiration album." I count hunnits on da table/twenties on da floor/fresh out of work, on the way to get sum mo/and I luv it/ and I luv it....." After Skeet caught his sale, he walked up to Pary'on with a dap & embrace. He then passed Pary'on a blunt he was smoking on. "Where the fuck you been, out with a lil bitch or something? Hell no. I over slept Man! I've missed so much calls". Skeet just shook his head. "Leave your car on. I'm about to go to the store. You want anything?" Damn I forgot to go to the store. Get me something to drink and some chips, hot pockets, all types of junk, I'm hungry. "Alright". Pary'on went inside his pocket to pull out a twenty dollar to give Skeet, but Skeet waved him off. "What you want is chump change broh. I'll be back and Pary'on began walking towards the trap spot. So much clientele was walking out the front door passing Pary'on. Some acknowledging him because they knew him. Once he made it to the door he almost walked into a smoker name Sherry. "Damn my bad Sherry. "No it's okay. That's my fault. Have a good day Pary'on. "You too, oh I will". "He laughed at her strong southern accent. White women had it the worst. Everybody in the house got happy when Pary'on came in. The front room was packed with his friends. Some were playing the X-box 360 game, called Off Duty, others were waiting for their turn, talking shit about one particular homeboy T.J. that keeps killing everyone. Guns were by their owners, along with scales to weigh out their product along with large amounts of weed, cocaine, X-pills, heroine & pain pills, everywhere on the table, floor, parts of the couch as well. A case of Bud Light was standing up with the box open. Pary'on walked by everyone dapping them up as some talk shit screaming for him to get the fuck out of the way of their game. He stopped in front of the case of beer to see it was only a few left. "Some more in the fridge broh "Blackie said word, and Pary'on walked into the kitchen where it was crowed with ten or more homies. They were shouting at the TV in the kitchen. It was a good bloody match going on the game fight night round 3. Muhammad Ali vs Joe Frazier. As he dapped everyone he opened the oven door to see a book bag he placed in there the prior night. He placed it on the counter next to the stove to retrieve the items out of it. First came out a 17 round 9 millimeter berretta, he placed it down on the counter, then he pulled out a brick of cocaine and a box of sandwich bags, then a jar of purple haze, marijuana, counting three pounds, and two big freezer bags tha contained mid-grade weed inside. Then lastly a freezer bag of X-pills. He plugged his phone charger inside the outlet next to the stove. He plugged his phone up then went through the contacts to a sale he knew he could count on for his hunger. He pressed the send button on his phone and the number began ringing, seconds later a unfamiliar voice answered the phone. "Welcome to Dominos, may I take your order? "Yes, is Brenda working? "She sure is, would you like to speak with her instead? "Yes please, if you don't mind. "It's no problem. Hold on for me." Pary'on could hear the phone being slightly covered as he heard the white girl call out to Brenda. Moments later Brenda's voice was heard. "This is Brenda. "What it do Bee? "Oh what's up Pee? What can II get you? "Hold on. "Pary'on put his phone down to scream out to his homies. "Do yall want something from Domino's while I'm getting something? All types of orders flew out. Pary'on picked the phone back up. Rudy came flying in the kitchen from the living room. "We want the same shit broh. That will kill that. We gonna eat it anyway. "Pary'on nodded his head, "just bring me ten large pizzas, a lot of cinnamon sticks, wings and a lot of sauce. I got you. "Alright, I'll send Malcom to deliver it, and I want coke this time. Not all weed. "Gotcha". "Give me an hour to be to you." Ten-four, "Click....That's how it went and minutes later Skeet came back from the store with more beer, blunts,cigarettes and with junk food for Pary'on. He stopped when he seen Pary'on to give him his keys and his bag of junk. He threw the bag on the counter to search through goodies. One of his homies ran to his side being nosey, "blunts," Pary'on passed him a box of swisher sweets. "Oh, Gummi lifesavers, let me get some. "Rudy said from his other side. Pary'on gave Rudy the bag. He then grabbed the bag of Funyons to eat. "Pass me a beer Skeet, "Lil Rico asked him. "Me too broh". Skeet stood in the refrigerator door passing out fresh cold beers. Everyone begin using blunts to roll up fresh weed. Pary'on phone began blowing up with back to back sales. Sales were coming through the front door, and the back door. Then at 3:45 p.m. Pary'on knew Sony Erricson mp 3 phone rang. Not too many people had this number. He answere it. "Hey how are you doing?" A soft sweet voice said on the other end. It was Marie. "Oh what's up baby? Just in this trap spot. What you just got from school?" "Yeah." "You got any homework?" "I did it while I was in school. "Don't lie. I don't play that shit. You're my girl, so you can't be no dummy. "No, I promise, I did it in school". Alright so what's up? I miss you today. I thought about you all day." "Fosho." Hold on baby. "Pary'on other phones were going off. He began answering them. Marie sat patiently just listening as Pary'on had her on hold for ten minutes. Pary'on finally picked up. "Hello," Yeah I'm still here. He loved her soft sweet voice." So what did you learn today in school? As Marie explained, Pary'on caught sales, but he never stop istening. He was falling for her, but, the streets had his heart. After about an hour on the phone, Pary'on asked her, "So you don't have friends you talk to on the phone?" "Yeah, I have some friends but, then she paused, "but, if you want me to go, I'll go. "Now Pary'on felt kind of bad. He gave in. "Alright if you want to stay on the phone and trap with me, then you can. But, I have to get this money ok. "Okay. And that's how it was. Marie would be on hold for twenty minutes at times, but every time Pary'on picked up the phone, "you there." She was always there. That made Pary'on smiled. She use to know some of his sales names, and all. Pary'on stayed on the phone with Marie all day & night on the block unless she was in school. It got to the point where he would be on the phone with her, until it was time for her to go to school with Pary'on. She loved being with him on the block. It was like they were always together. And that attracted Pary'on love and attention to the fullest. He Love his Marie, and Marie loved her Pary'on.

CHAPTER 2

Back To the Future

———— ✦ ————

Pary'on pulled up to the school attracting all the attention. Everyone knew who Poncho & Nae Nae, father was including teachers. Paty'on had his coolness about him. A lot of people were drawn to him. You could tel he's been through some shit. And from the looks of it, he came out victorious. He stayed fresh as a man can 24/7. Always had on fresh out the box kicks. And straight off the rack of clothes. And he matched from head to toe. Staying color coordinated, as he approached the kids pick up section at the school, he notices Poncho's energy level. "Whats's happening"! He said to both of them. "Hi daddy!" Nae Nae said. As he stood in front of Poncho with his hands out for him to dap up, Poncho dapped him softly. "What's wrong?" My stomach hurt!" Than Nae Nae spoke up. "He sick." Pary'on did notice that Poncho was dragging dismorning. But, he thought he just didn't wake up fully. I guess mama knows huh. That's why he had to pick up Poncho prescription. Then the teacher stuck her hand out. Pary'on shook it. "Good morning ma'am. How are you?" I'm fine Mr. Pary'on." What's wrong with my boy?" "He has been throwing up and using the bathroom all day. The nurse contacted Ms. Marie." "OK, Thank you." And once inside the car Pary'on turned the music down so Poncho could relax. Once they got to Marie's job Nae Nae looked out the window, "we at mommies job! "yep." They all got out with Pary'on carrying Poncho. His boy was sick. When they all walked inside the clinic where Marie worked it was packed. Marie notices her family walking up to the front desk. A smile came across her face; she walked from behind the desk. She approached Pary'on. He bent down to meet his wifey for a kiss. She rubbed Poncho on his back. "You gonna be okay baby! As soon as I come home, I'll tend to you okay." Poncho just shook his head slightly with his arms around Pary'on neck and his head on Pary'on shoulder. "Hey Nae Nae." "Hey mommy. I love you mommy." "I love you too." Marie looked at Pary'on. "Hold on baby. "She walked bacj behind the desk to retrieve Poncho prescription., Her co-workers loved seeing Marie & Pary'on together. They completed each other. Pary'on watched his wifey smiling up, snickering something to her co-workers. Then he heard Marie say "Girl bye!" Marie stopped in front of Pary'on to hand him the prescription. She grabbed his hand to walk him and the kids out to the car. She stopped to her car to retrieve something. She hit the alarm button to deactivate the alarm on her 2017 Black on Black Range Rover. Her Christmas gift from Pary'on. She came out with a bottle of ice breaker cube chewing gum. She then walked across the parking lot towards her family. Pary'on was just finishing placing Poncho in the car. Marie walked up to him so close he could feel her heart beat. She stuck her hand inside his waistline, then sliding her arm inside his pants to his massive dick. He bent down to kiss her. As they stuck their tongues down each other's throat, Pary'on grabbed a hand full of her soft ass. They continue for a few seconds until Marie bit down on his lip. "You better stop. "You are the one. "Then she exhaled a long deep breath. "I can't wait to get home daddy." "Daddy can't wait either." "Well, I love you. I better get back inside." "I love you too Bae. Marie wallked to the car door and stuck her head inside to tell the kids bye. Pary'on walked up behind his bulge in front of his jeans all over her ass. When she stood up she backed her ass up against him hard. He bent back down to get one last peck on Marie lips." Text you in a little bit." "Alright bae." As Marie was walking off he slapped her ass hard. "Owwww! Bighead!" And she flipped him off. "That's what I want you to do!" And Marie kissed her hand then slapped her ass. "I do that enough!" And Marie laughed out loud waving to him as she walked up the steps to enter the door to her job. As he made his way to the Pharmacy to fil Poncho's prescription his mind drifted back to 2006........

CHAPTER 3

Back 2 da Basics

———————— ❧ ————————

Pary'on got dressed in a pair of evisu jeans, evisu t-shirt, and bathing apple sneakers. He was going to see Yung Joc, T.I., Playa Circle, and Yo Gotti in concert. He really wanted to see Yo Gotti. He was talking to Marie on the phone as he put on all his jewerly. You better be good tonight Pary'on." "I am, trust me." "I do. You just a little to excited right now." "The whole city gonna be out there." "And you need to be careful." "I will." So, I'm not gonna hear from you no more tonight?" "I'll call you when I get back into the house." "okay." "Okay I love you." "I love you too." Click.....The whole team got up at Al's spot to leave out for the big concert. The concert was at the North Charleston Coliseum. Once they arrived they got inside quick. They all were high and gone off x-pills. Playa Circle hit the stage wth Duffle bag boi. Then Yo Gotti performed, "Back to the Basics. I got em, among some other songs. Yung Joc rapped, I know you see it, Dope boy magic, going down, and T.I. closed the show with 24's lets get away, some off his Trap music album, then the king album," You can have whatever you like, finish the concert. It was now 1 o'clock. They decided that they should hit the strip club: Badda Bing. Pary'on went back to the block with the othe niggas that did not go to the concert. He called Marie. "She picked up on the 4th ring. But, she did not sound sleepy period. Damn! What were you doing? Why you ain't been asleep? Because I'm use to talking to you every night before

I go to sleep and I was worried about you." That made him smile. "I was thinking about you lil mama. "I love you. I love you too Marie. Hold on. "Pary'on had to be on point around this side of town. The police was bad around there. He picked the phone up once he got on the interstate I-26, it was packed. The concert brought the whole city out seems like. "Hello baby." "Yeah, did you enjoy the concert?" "Yeah it was straight. What were you doing the whole time daddy was gone?" "Well Daddy, all I did was think of you. I talked to my best friend about you. "And he listened to her talk for a while. He made it to the block in record time. Rudy, Skeet and Moose was the only ones inside playing the game. "Boy yall need to leave again!" "Skeet said proudly. "Hell yeah." We cake up tonight." "Rudy agreed. Moose added, "I'll be sleeping here tonight. Pary'on looked at him in surprise. "Why!" What happened? "I refused to go get my gal from work. I sent a junkie to pick her up. Now she shittin. I told her the money was coming to fast. "Marie listened at how they were talking and wondered if Pary'on would let a junkie come get her. But, she didn't ask him. Then they took turns catching sales as Pary'on stayed on the phone in the kitchen by himself in the dark talking to Marie. The backdoor to the house leading into the kitchen was open.

Pary'on sat in a chair leaning back against the stove looking outside in the backyard when he seen a person in the bushes across the fence along -the ditch. He sat there watching. This was not normal. He watched closer in the dark kitchen. Then he seen them had on ski-masks. He put the phone down as Marie continued to talk, when one of the masked individuals jumped over the fence with his hands on the top and his feet never touching the anything, clearing it. He ran out the door gun blazing. The first gunshot struck the mask man. Then the mask man tried jumping back over the fence, but Pary'on let him have it. Pary'on let off 9 more shots trying to hit the other masked individual that did not hop the fence yet. But, that individual returned fire of his own. His shots were off target. Pary'on could see the sparks the bullets were making as they ricocheted off the fence, and other things. Then Pary'on heard a window's glass shatter behind him. He ran back inside running into Rudy and Skeet. I've got t the fuck out of here! The police is going to be coming! "Everybody began scrambling, grabbing all the incriminating evidence as possible. Pary'on grabbed the phone he was talking to Marie on. "Hell" "What happen?" I'll call you later! I love you! Before Marie could answer she heard a dial tone. She knew something was up.. And as she knew those were not firecrackers she heard in Pary'on's background. She tried calling his phone back, but she got no answer. She began crying as they tried their best to clean up any evidence, then they heard sirens. "Let's go! Come on! "Rudy jumped in the car with Pary'on and Skeet and Moose rode together. Once Pary'on backed out he saw the police cars turning on the street. "Shit!" He drove forward slowly. Not trying to peel out, but Skeet did not think like that. He went hauling ass in front of Pary'on. Pary'on backed up into the yard across from them turning the other way. He gunned it then. The police tried stopping Skeet, but Skeet pulled into a yard driving past them, then got back on the road. All the police tried to go after Skeet. Then one gunned it forwarded to the direction Pary'on went. Pary'on knew Greenhurst had four entrances to the neighborhood, so he decided to go for the last one. Before he turned on the street to go to the last entrance, he seens the police finally turned behind him. "Oh I got you bitch!" Pary'on floored it. It was another Greenhurst neighborhood across from the one they were in, but they would have to cross the main mile-Jamison road highway. He got up to 125 miles per hour hitting small curves that twisted the straight ahead street. The cops car behind him could not be seen anymore, and he was coming up to the entrance as he was approaching, approximately 100 feet away three cops cars flew past going towards the head of the neighborhood without slowing down. Now going 140 miles per hour he gunned it across the highway into the other Greenhurst, not even caring if oncoming cars were coming. He turned down Carmen street. He stopped to the best of his ability as the car skidded as he hit the brakes to turn into a yard. The car began fish tailing but Pary'on held on to it. The car stopped at a jerking stop.

Pary'on then made his way to the backyard behind the abandoned house shutting off the car. He looked over at Rudy who looked as if he was gonna have a heart attack. Rudy eyes were popping out his head, and he was breathing heavy. Everything around them was so quiet, except for the police sirens that got so loud now because it was a bunch of them on the scene. After they sat in silence not even moving or breathng too hard for the next ten minutes that seemed like an eternity. Pary'on looked at Rudy with a sly grin. "They both bust out laughing." Then they dapped up. "Boy you did that! Rudy said smiling. "Hell yeah!" I wonder if Skeet straight. Rudy's look said it all. Pary'on grew up with Skeet his whole life. He knew Skeet to be smarter than the move he pulled a while ago. Pary'on "voice grew loud with disbelief." I hope my nigga okay. Damn! Moose just had a baby too. I got faith! I hoped them niggas straight." Then they both jumped out of fear as Pary'on's phone rang loud cracking the slient night. He answered fast. "Yo." It was T.J. and Blackie. "Man what the fuck is going on in the hood?" "Where you at!" I'm passing by now. Every entrancr got police cars blocking the exits and entrance. And in the front the police are all up and down the street. It is even some with no lights on across the street in the other Greenhurst. Pary'on got paranoid when he sat across the street to the other Greenhurst. Rudy could hear Blackie and T.J. what happen and he told him where he was. "Well you better not move because it is lit up like Christmas downtown, Summerville. Cal me if yall need me. "Okay, 10-4...." Click....Pary'on pulled his seat bac, got comfortabe, then he rolled him a blunt. "You may as we roll your own Rudy, because I'm not passing this. "And Rudy did just that, pulling the passenger side seat back to lean too. Halfway into the blunt Pary'on turned the car on to flip out the tv deck. he put the movie "Belly" inside the DVD player on the 9 inch monitor. When the scene was of Nas and T-Box talking about where he was all night came on, Pary'on called Marie. She was awake. She answered on the second ring. "Hello baby! She answered jittery. "What's up baby!" "What happen to you!" And he explained as he just explaining like it was a normal thing. Marie knew that she had a man really deep into the streets. Rudy grabbed his cellphone and called his girl too. Marie started crying. "Don't ever scare me like that! I was worried sick!" He just let her ler it all out. "I'm sorry baby. It won't happen like that again. Not that way. I can promise you that. I won't get into any more trouble like that. But, I can promise you I'm do everything in my will power to stay clear from danger. Sometime shit be coming my way baby. Like tonight it was out of nowhere, but it makes me feel good to hear you crying over me. I have never had a female care for me like that. It will get better. Trust me. "I hope so." I don't want anything to happen to you before we meet. I already told my mother about you. "Stop lyin! And what she said?" "Along as I am happy and I told her you made me happy. "Damn that's what's up. I love you Marie. "I love you too, Please don't hang up on me like that. i was scared I lost the only thing I love. And she was crying hard when she said it. He just listene to her cry for a while. Then he started being real open about love. She loved him even more after that because she felt she was real. After a few hours of talking, Pary'on looked over at Rudy who was facing the window snoring lightly. He checked the time, it was 5:45 a.m. He rolled another blunt and fired it up. He cranked up the car and backed out the backyard. He looked at the grass in front of the yard and seen big muddy tire streaks all through the yard. He put his car in drive after he seen it was clear on both ends of Carmen Street. He made it to the entrance he drove across, and he went the opposite way from the hood. He made it to the lakes of Summerville neighborhood and used the cut to get on the other side of town to a whole different county. Now that he was out Dorchester County, he felt safer. Now in Charleston County, he decided to go to his cousin Leroy house. He just sat in the driveway. Leroy car was in the driveway, so he was most defintely home. "Baby I'm call you back. I'm at my cousin's house. I'm safe. Let me make a few calls around to check up on my people, then I'll get back with you. Get some sleep. It's gonna be a while baby." You sure your gonna be okay?" "Fo'sho. I love you." "I love you more. Okay, you be safe." "I got you." Now Pary'on breathe out in relief. He had more drugs and in his car that could of got him an easy life sentence. He had to get everyone's work that belong to them. He made a sacrifice for his niggas because his niggas would of done the same. He only did what he did out of loyalty. As he looked up, he notice someone looking out Leory's living room window blinds. All he seen was a finger holding the blinds up. But the finger had a long manicured french tip nail on it. Then about five minutes later the front door opened, and a big king Rottweiler came out along with the female in a silk robe. She was smoking a cigarette. She was a Filipino, Asian looking beautiful woman with long hair put inside a sloppy bun. She sat on the chair on the porch. The front door remained open then Leroy appeared in a fresh looking tank top with grey sweat pants on with some leather house slippers. He still had his door open and his waves in tack. That's when Pary'on opened the car door. "I was wondering when your ass was going to get out the car and come in the house. "Leroy said ighting his cigarette. Pary'on got out, and stretched cracking his muscles, and screamed out. "Ahhhh shit!" What the fuck happen to your car?" "What are you talking about!?" Pary'on ran to the other side but was met by a vicious growl." The dog stop in mid-stride to run to his master's feet lying down. Pary'on was happy it was only dirt, because his rims were filled with grass with chunks of dirt. "I'll tell you this, it was a long night.

"It looks like it was Reese my cousin Pary'on. Pary'on my girl Maurice. We call her Reese. "She got up to shake his hand, and give him a hug. "Nice to meet some of the family, even under weird circumstances. "Nice to meet you too." He was about to explain, then he looked at Reese then Leroy. "She kool!" "He asked Leory pointing at Reese. "Oh yeah. She real solid. Then he explained. "Well looks like I'll go get breakfast on for four now, well five. I can't forget about my king baby. Come on king. "The king looked up at Leroy with a sad look. "Get your ass in the house boy. Pary'on sat down in the chair. Reese just sat, as him and Leroy talke more. "You can't be driving that car cus." "I know." "My partner has a used car lot. How much you trying to spend? I know he got a few Cadillac's, Nissans, Benezes, Jags and Crown Vics all used." "Anywhere between a grand and less. Well he gotcha. We will go out there later. In the meantime yall come on inside. "And Pary'on went to wake Rudy up. Rudy looked around crazy. "Man, come on broh, we safe and bring all the work inside, all of it. We good over here. Pary'on grabbed his bags of work, and went inside. Leroy had a nice brick house inside a well off neighborhood inside of North Charleston. Rudy still did not know where he was. He knew he was in a very nice neighborhood due to the houses on Leroy's street. Once inside Reese directed Rudy to the back of the house to Leroy's man cave. As Rudy looked around he notice Leroy had taste. When he got to the man cave it was no doubt about it. Leroy was a huge Dallas Cowboys fan. Leroy turned his Playstation 2 on. Then John Madden footbakk came on the screen. "Which one of yall going to lose first?" Leroy asked." I know you ain't talking shit. Nigga I've been beating your ass in video games since we were young niggas. "Give me the remote. I'ma fuck your ass up. "Minutes into the game they were yelling like they were watching real football. Pary'on picked the Indianopolis Colts because Peyton Manning is his favorite quarterback ever. Deion neon Sanders is his favorite player of all time also Randy Moss! By the time the fourth quarter started, Leroy was up by ten. Pary'on got the ball off a fumble, but, couldn't run it back. So now it was three minutes left. "You can't do nothing, but throw the ball nigga! Watch, he throw the ball to Marvin Harrison or Reggie Wayne Rudy! Pary'on press the x button on the Playstation controller to hike the ball. The letters, numbers, and other symbols appeared on top of the players, and Pary'on seen Leroy sent double coverage on both Reggie Wayne and Marvin Harrison. So he threw the ball to the running back Joseph Addai. And Joseph Addai ran for twenty-one yards. "Yeah nigga1" You see it! Pary'on press the no huddle offense x button multiple times. He pressed the x button fast to hike the ball then threw the ball to Dallas Clark their tight end. Dallas Clark ran the ball for an extra fifteen yards. After an eights yard catch, Leroy started screaming. "Oh! You throw it again nigga! I'm picking that shit off!" And they both went through their playbooks. Pary'on picked a HB toss play to Joseph Addai. He first made it look as if he was picking a pass play than at the line of scrimmage he switch the play to a HBs toss. He was on Leroy's forty-three yard line, so he almost in field goal range. So he would score regardless. But, he was going for the end zone. He hike the ball and Joseph Addai ran for thirteen yards. The next play when Pary'on hiked the ball, Leroy sacked him and he fumbled, but he recovered the bakk and for four yards out of the play. Leroy defense tightened all the way up.It was now third and nine. Pary'on tried a play for the end zone, and Leroy batted the ball down. Intercep the ball, don't bat it down! Leroy screamed. Paryon went for the field goal, and got it. He was now down by seven witha little over two minutes to go." It's over nigga! I'ma run the time out on your ass! Pary'on kicked the ball off and Leroy ran it back to his own forty-nine yard line. "Oh yeah nigga! If I score now it's over fo'sho muthafucka!" "You ain't bout to do shit nigga! Watch this!" Pary'on went with a goal line defensive play, and Leroy faked him and threw the ball, a short pass, and ran the ball seven yards. Two minute warning and Leroy begin running the ball on Pary'on trying t run rhe clock out. Pary'on begins using his timeouts. Third down with one minute, and fifteen seconds, that's alll the time left on the clock. Leroy hiked the ball and he ran it. Pary'on press the square button to change players to be the player close to the football player who had the ball, and he recovered the ball. He ran the ball. Then Dwight Freeway was runnin the ball Madden screamed. "He could go all the way!" But Dwight Freeway was slow. Pary'on was running diagonally across the field to avoid getting tackled. But Leroy dived, and caught Dwight Freeway on the twenty-one yard line. "Yeah nigga!" "Pary'on screamed. You still down by seven! You have to score nigga! And it is thirty-eight seconds left. What you going to do nigga with one damn timeout left?" "I'm going in the pussy nigga! That's where I'm going! "Well we will see! They both were on their feet standing in front of the television. Pary'on picked his play then hiked the ball. Nothing! "Yeah nigga, three more downs to go! Lcroy taunted Pary'on. The next play, a thirteen yard pass, and Marvin Harrison ran out of bounds. Twenty more seconds. Pary'on hiked the ball, and short pass to Jeff Saturday for five yards. Thiurteen seconds. Pary'on tried to run the ball in but got tackle within the goal line. He tried using his last timeout, but it took extra seconds. It was third and goal with four seconds left. The ball was one yard away for a touchdown. "It all comes down to this play nigga! What you gonna do?! "Don't worry about that!" Peyton Manning hiked the ball and it was a quarterback sneak, then Pary'on pressed the square button for the quarterback to dive forward. "TOUCHDOWN! INDY! DAMN Right! Touchdown!" "Oh shit! Its tied nigga! You won't survive overtime!" "We'll see! And it was time for pary'on to pick his play. Either go for the extra point or go for the two point conversion. And he thought about it. "Man fuck it! I'm going for the win! "Yeah that's what you do my nigga!" And Pary'on went for two. "Oh this nigga got balls huh! Peyton Manning hiked the ball, and threw it in the end zone. Pary'on screamed. "It's good! It's Over! It's OVER nigga!" Reese came running inside he room, she was smiling looking at her man. "Baby he is so fucking lucky!" And they both explained what happen. She was smiling looking back-n-fourth at both of them as they both explain their version of the game. She just walked off back to the kitchen, shaking her head smiling. She had the whole house smelling good. "Go ahead and play Rudy, I'm going to help wifey with breakfast. Your very lucky nigga! It's because you're a guest." "I don't want to hear that shit nigga! Fuck overtime! Ain't no pressure on Peyton nigga! P-money nigga! P-money is the best quarterback ever nigga! "Please! And Leroy went to the kitchen. Pary'on grabbed his phone to call Skeet, and it went to the voicemail. Pary'on shook his head. "What happen!" Man that nigga shit going straight to the voicemail. I'ma try Moose. "I already tried. His shit off, or dead too. Pary'on thought of who he could call to get in contact with these niggas, becaue if he could not get in contact with them niggas he doubt anybody else could either. So he decided to call Moose gal's job. He dialed 411 information in his cell. "What city and state"! Summerville, South Carolina. "What location!" Subway off Mainstreet." Hold on. "Seconds past, "the number 851-0003. Press one for direct calll, for any other assistance press two. "Pary'on pressed one. Then the phone started ringing on the fourths ring the line picked up.

"This is Chell speaking, may I help you place an order? Chell this is Pee. "What's up Pee? Where is your fucking husband?" At his mama house. He sure could not come home to me after coming home 8:15 in the morning talking about he ran from the police! That nigga back to his old ways." No, he is for real! Man, shit went down last night. So Pary'on explained what happen except for he was the one that shot the masked man."Well damn, all yall alright?" I'm trying to find Skeet. "Well i don't know about Skeet, but Moose right over there at his mama's house. He better be! "Alright, good looking. Alright bye. "Bye." Pary'on looked at Rudy, so what's up? Moose at his mama's house. He told Chell he ran from the police and Chell thought he was a bitch. So I'm about to call over there now. "Rudy shook his head yeah. Pary'on called to the house, and his sister keytah answered. Hello." "Wake that nigga ass up." Then Pary'on heard Keytah waking him up. "Get your ass up, Pary'on on the phone!" Here nigga! And you better get your puppy! He has this living room stink and he bit up my Airmax!" Then Moose answered. "Yo", in a very groggy,sleepy voice. "Man get your ass up nigga! You got me and Rudy worried sick about yall ass! Where is Skeet?" I don't know. "How did yall get away?:" How we got away? Aww man! Let me tell you! "Please tell me. Pary'on asked smiling. "This damn nigga Skeet seen that we had no win high speeding the way we went. So as we turned off of Roberts, three police cruisers were coming towards us. So this nigga says, we have to jump out! And he slows down some and he said jump! We both jumped out. The car flew past me jerking me a little. We hit the grass, but we was up like cats. We ran together hopping fences! The police shot at us as we were hoping fences! "What the fuck! "Yeah! Then we ran to Wendy! On Wendy we ran into a truck drive's garage. We closed the backyard door to the garage! His dog was barking loud as hell at the kitchen door, the door to gets into the garage! Skeet started calling truck driver's phone! No answer! But, the dog is going crazy! We tried kissing at him, calling his name, but that made him act crazier! So we just looked out the back door! The police was all over! As we looked between houses onto the other street, you could see the police everywhere! Bright lights on their cars! And police on foot with flashlights! After a while we heard truck driver yelling at his dog to shut up! We start knocking at the kitchen door screaming his name! We heard truck driver scream, what the fuck! But, he opened the door after he got his dog under control. We explained what was going on! But, he did not care once we gave him seven grams of hard.

He just started smoking crack lookin out the window at the police! That boys house stink just like that truck! He keep that dog with him! After covering our noses seemed like forever, Skeet went in the backyard for fresh air, and notice no police cruisers riding around! So we got truck driver to take us to Sherry house! Me and Skeet ran inside the back of the truck, and we waited for truck driver to hurry up, and take us! So we closed the curtains to the bed area of the truck and peaked out to the road as truck driver drove! We see Skeet's car being towed! Once we got to the entrance we seen the police asked him to down the window! Then the officer ask hi, did you notice any strange activity hour's ago? We are looking for a few suspects that fled the scene on foot! "I seen a group of fellas back on Lisa Drive just snooping in the backyard, but I think that youngin in that house is a little whore if you know what I mean. It's always young fellas over there. But, besides that I mosey on along by my lonesome. Me and old Daisy here. Ain't that right Daisy? And Daisy srtarted barking. Then the police said well, good day Sir and safe driving. And he dropped us off at Sherry's and Sherry bought me over here after my bitch started flipping out about the time. Her and Skeet left me here. "Moose was so tired he could just fall back to sleep on the phone. "Well I'm trying to find him. At least I know he got away too. Well, tell him to call me if you hear from him. We have to meet up on common grounds. I'm sending everyone a text message to meet me at my house at one o'clock. "Well I'm about to get some sleep until then." "Alright." One." One." Rudy looked at Pary'on and shook his head smiling. That shit crazy!" Tell me about it. I'm about send out these text messages." Then minutes later, Leroy called them into the kitchen to fix themselves some food, when they got inside the kitchen the aroma was so thick. When Pary'on walked to the stove he notice that Reese had mountains of food in pans, pots and on plates. Reese and leroy was sitting at the table with big plates of food. "Eat up. I made enough. "Reese instructed them." Thank you Reese. "Pary'on said washing his hands inside the sink. 'Word. "Rudy added. Pary'on grabbed a big plate. A paper plate brand that was a thick heavy paper plate made for cookouts. He loaded rhe plate up. "Those eggs, salmon, cheese, tater tots are Filipino styled cooked. I hope yall like them. "Reese let them know, I'm about to fuck this shit up Reese!" Pary'on told her. Reese got them big cups of Filipino mixed juice drink. After ten minutes they were up for seconds. "Reese, you are officially my cousin for damn sho! You did that girl! I'm come eat over here all the time! She just laughed out loud. "Thank you for your approval. I try. Fuck trying girl, you are the best! This is the best food I taste in a real long time! Then Leory butted in. "Cause you've been in jail nigga!" "And everybody start laughing. "Fuck you! Boy i know damn good cooking when I taste it! And this is on another level family! That's for damn sure!" Rudy adding stuffing his mouth as he fixed another plate. "Yeah you use to it nigga. "Reese laughed out so loud, she covered her mouth laughing crying at Pary'on. Well I'm glad yall like it. "Like! We love it!" They stayed at the table talkin with full bellies. Leroy called his partner to find out what kind of cars he had. "I just got a 2004 BMW 750i, 2001 Lincoln Town Car, 2003 Lincoln Navigator, 2000 Lincoln Contenential and 2005 CLK Benz." "Well, we about to come by." Okay buddy. I'll see you in a few." Bet." Click....Leroy got dress and they waited for Reese. Once Reese got to the car they all left to buy a car. Once at the car lot Pary'on saw that he passes this place all the time. It was not big at all, but he had a nice collection. Before they exited out Leroy's Honda Accord, a short stocky Carcausian male came out the small trailer office to greet them. He was dressed in Khaki shorts, sperry boat shoes and a white short sleeve button down shirt that was tucked inside his waistband. He smiled walking up to the car. Once Leroy got out he stuck his hand out for Leroy to shake it. "Leroy, Pauly." "how are you my friend?" "I'm okay Pauly. I bought my cousin here to buy something. Let me introduce yall. Pauly meet my cousin Pary'on. Pary'on my friend Pauly. "Pauly walked up to Pary'on with his hand out. Pary'on shook his hand. "What's going on Pauly?" Nothing man. So you want one of these lemons I got, or you want a winner?" "Definitely a winner!" "Oh where are my manners, how are you maam?" "I'm ok." "And you Sir! He said sticking a hand out to Rudy. Rudy shook his hand nodding his head. "May I ask how you will be paying for the car Pary'on? Always CASH! COD...Cash on deck!" "My kind of guy. Well lets get down to business to find something out here and come let me know something. Let me speak to you Leroy. "And the two men excused themselves. And Reese, Pary'on and Rudy looked at the 2004 BMW il 750. "Leroy I can tell money a mile away. He's a big fish out the street pond." "He is." "Well tell him to bring his friends to me. Do he got any coke?" "He sure do. He don't got none with him. But he got plenty of that." "Good, let me know I'm good to deal with. And tell him to come back with some before we do any other dealing. "Alright." We will be back." And Leroy walked off and joined Reese and Pary'on. Rudy was looking at a car himself. "He want some coke." Surprised Pary'on said, "Word!" He said he don't want to deal no business until you come back with some coke. "Well lets go back to your spot. "They left, and was back in forty-five minutes. When they pulled up this time Pauly waved for them to come inside. They all went inside. Pauly begin using his finger to rub his nose as he twitched. "I cleared house so we can have our privacy. You got some good shit?" "The best in the streets." And Pary'on casually went inside his pocket to retrieve an ounce of the best coke he had. As he passed it to Pauly, Pauly whistled. Pauly untied the sandwich bag to chip off the one ounce block of solid coke. He used a car key to dig into the soft but firm block of coke. He took a one on one up each nostril. He passed gas seconds later as the good quality of coke hit his stomach. He gave himself another one on one up each nostril. He then got up to peek out the window. When he sat down his jaws were twitching. "You like that Beamer don't you?" "I do." Well give me two more these and three grand..." I'll be be back. I told you Rudy I needed to bring more. Good thing I listen to my gut. Hold on Pauly. "Pary'on left to go out to the car. When he came back inside he had his book bag. He pulled out his triple bean digital scale and weighed out fifty-six grams. He placed it all in one big sandwich bag. he then counted out three grand. "Here you go." Pary'on gave Pauly everything. Pauly went into his khaki shorts pocket to retrieve the BMW keys. "We will be great business partners doing business like this."

"I don't handle it no other way. "And Pary'on signed al the proper paperwork and he placed the pen down. Pauly gave him some dealer tags to put on. Pary'on drove off with Rudy in the car behind Leroy. He called Leroy on his phone. "Stop at he next gas station. And he seen Leroy moving over toward the exit to get off the main highway. Pary'on gave Leroy his keys to the Grand Marquis. I'll come get it." Then Rudy spoke yo, I'll ride with them. I'll meet you at your house. "And Leroy gave Rudy the keys. Rudy went inside the gas station to get something to drink. And Pary'on walked up to Leroy with a hand full of cash. "Good looking cuz. "No problem." Just be safe out here. You just got home. "No doubt." They dapped up, and Pary'on left. He went to the tint shop first to tint his fishbowl windows. Pary'on looked down at his G shock watch to see it was 12:40 p.m. He was gonna be late to his own gathering. But he had to tint these windows. When he pulled up to his neighborhood, he notice a familiar car turn on his street. When he finally got to the stop sign to turn on his street, he notices everyone was there. And that familiar car pulled into the grass of his yard. He looked at his watch 1:20 p.m. He pulled into his driveway behind Blackie's car. He hopped out his Beamer to all eyes on his new car. "Well damn cux thats how you do? Go get a new car and shit. After a rough night with the police. Those 24" won't fit on that pretty muthafucka! "His cousin David said dappin him up checking out the nice toy. Then Skeet jumped out that familiar looking car with an ace bandage wrap around his wrist and elbow on his right arm. Skeet was smiling at Pary'on. Skeet and Pary'on really were right-hand men. But, never made the feeling real. But everyone knows how they felt about each other. "Ain't no smiling bruh!" "Yeah i know you could of called somebody. What! You can't call nobody?" If Martin Lawerence would have been there, he would have been very proud and jealous of Pary'on. "Jerome Impersonation. They started laughing. They tapped arms due to Skeet's injury. Everyone was sitting outside waiting on Pary'on or Skeet to pull up. Skeet had a key to Pary'on house and Pary'on had a key to Skeet's house. "Let's get this family meeting on the way. "Pary'on said opening the door for everyone to come inside. Once everyone was inside and Pary'on turned the alarm off the house, it was time to get down to business. "Well, well,well." I'ma tell everybody why I did what I did last night. "Pary'on explained what happen about him shooting the masked man. "I was not giving those niggas the chance to hurt none of my brothers. I got some of the work, Rudy got some and whatever Moose and Skeet got. "We came to the conclusion man, fuck that spot. We never have to go there again or get anything from there. It's a loss. As long as none of us was hurt, or got locked up, we won. All that shit can be replaced. I have the newspaper right here and it is on the front page. Unsolved Homicide: had to be drug related. Masked man dead on the scene. Also was wanted for four armed robberies, multiple drug offenses, etc. Police is looking for any suspects, possibly the suspect that fleds the scene in a dark colored car on big rims and the suspect that stole the impounded 2001 Buick Park Avenue. Any information, contact crime stoppers, 555-1111, or call your local police department...Bum said reading the paper section to everyone. Everyone looked at Pary'on. "Looks like yougot your first body fast just coming home." Skeet chanted squeezing Pary'on's shoulders. Big Six walked up to pary'on with a dap. Suave said, "thats my boy." I raised you well. "Pary'on flipped his cousin the middle finger. "So fuck that spot. Keytah is straight. The police already questioned her for hours. She already talked to the landlord. She will get everything out the house tomorrow Moose added. "In the meantime we chilling over here." Suave said turning on the TV with the remote control. The family meeting is adjourned...Then Pary'on, Rudy and Skeet begin giving everybody their individual bags of stuff....

CHAPTER 4

Mask on Mask off

The masked robber that got away was a nigga from the country named Mondo. Mondo sat in his living room drinking Hennessey from the bottle. His partner was gun down in his face last night. A lick gone bad. That was his robbing partner Blanks. Mondo and Blanks were down since the sandbox, now he is gone. Mondo looked at the news and read the newspaper all night. This was the second day. Blanks family, the one he did have in his corner was going crazy. They all were looking for him as if he done this to Blanks. Mondo was about to pull up to Blanks mama house to drop off fifteen thousand dollar for funeral arrangements or whatever else she needed. She was the only one of Blanks family member that did not think he actually did the murder himself. "It bothered him that people would even think that. Blanks was the only person he trusted like that. Mondo looked at the fifteen thousand dollars cash as if he was cheating Blanks. Blanks life meant more. "I'll get revenge for you bruh. Trust me, I will do something. This ain't gonna ride like this. "Mondo spoke out loud as if Blanks could of hear him. They knew them niggas was out at the concert. So the lick was suppose to be easy, at least that's what there leak told them. He trusted the leak to a certain extinct. But, the leak was a snake himself. He had to call the leak to find out what was going on. Mondo pulled out his phone and the leaks name in his contacts section. And on the third ring he answered. "Hold on Mondo." About a

21

minute later the leak was back on the phone. "Man! Yall fuck that lick up man!" "What!" It was over before it began! I thought nobody was supposed to be there! And all the work and money was supposed to be inside! It seems like that muthafucka was waiting on us! "Whoa, whoa, whoa! Hold up! So what you trying to say? Mondo had to be careful with his words, because he did not want to beef with this type of nigga. He needed this type of beast on his team. "All I'm saying is, before we even got over the fence shots rang out." "I know Pary'on just so happen to be chilling at the backdoor of the kitchen. Right place, wrong time." Mondo face balled up at the sound of Pary'on. He hated him. Oh pretty boy, who thinks he run shit. Mondo knew he slung iron, but he ddn't think he was a killer. So Pary'on fired at us like that! Damn sure did! Shit on edge right now. So niggas trying to find out what is what, and who is who. Your name ain't come around yet. But, when it do, I will call you to let you know something. I'm going after that nigga Pary'on! Fuck what you heard! He tried to kill me too! The leak smiled. "Ok check it. I'll tell you where he stay, but we all over here now. I'm down the street talking to you. I had to walk off. I'ma come spray that shit up! You need to leave! "Calm down! I got you, but when you strike, I want you to hit the spot too. So that is gonna take some planninf." "Yeah, we'll make that shit happen! Because my right-hand dead and gone. And these niggas walking around with their chest poking out." "Fo'sho. Well I'ma get off this phone, we will link up. Meet me at the game room tonight. "Bet. "Bet that." Click...Mondo shook his head at the thought Pary'on killing Blanks. He sure underestimated Pary'on. He knew he would shoot, but go for the kill was another thing. Mondo got in his Chevy Caprice to go to Blanks mothers house. He drank out the bottle of henny as he drove. He was on his third pack of Newport's that day. He got to Mrs. Jones house in twenty minutes. He parked in front of a fully packed yard.. A lot of Mrs. Jones friends and family have been keeping her company. As Mondo looked at the fully lit house he notices a black reef on the door. A lot of bugs flew around the light on the porch. Plenty of nights went by him and Blanks sat swatting at bugs on the porch, smoking weed when they were younger. He fought to control his tears. He reached over to the passenger seat to retrieve the crown royal bag full of the fifteen grand for Blanks funeral arrangements. He left his car on then exited the fully classic Chevy Caprice. As he mazed through the many cars in Mrs. Jones yard he slowly walked up to the four concrete steps to the front door. He rang the doorbell then knocked twice as he always did coming to this house to get Blanks to come outside to play for many of years when they were young kids. Seconds later a younger female voice asked, "Who is it!" "It's a friend, I have something to give Mrs. Jones for the funera arrangements." Hold on please." Then Mondo heard the female run off. Minutes later Mrs. Jones voice could be heard on the other side of the door. "Who is it?" "It's me mama." Mrs. Jones began unlocking the door quickly as she heard the name Mondo barley used to call her. When she opened the front door, Mondo stood looking at a very hurt woman. Otlher family members stoodd behind her lookin to see who was on the other side of the door. Mondo handed over the crown royal bag containing the fifteen thousand dolllars. Mrs. Jones just looked at Mondo for a second. Tears began rolling down Mondo's face onto Mrs. Jones shoulder as they held each other crying. The family members just watched on as tears began welding up at the sight of the hurt two people, who dearly missed Blanks. They held each other for ten minutes not saying a word. Then Mrs. Jones broke the embrace grabbing Mondo's face with both hands and looked him in the eye. It is gonna be okay baby! God called him home son! I love you! And don't you go out there doing anything stupid. Because no mother should feel the way I feesl! What's in the bag Mondo? Mondo looked down at the bag. "My brother's funeral arrangements Ma. Bury him right. He would have done the same for me. "Mondo heard some low voices, "bless his heart and thank you Jesus, from the family members in the back of Mrs. Jones. "Well, I'm about to go. I'll be front row. I love you. Mondo heard, "I love you too. "As he walked off back to his car, he did not even look back. He got inside his car to go to the Game Room to meet his mole. And once he got information he needed, he was gonna kill him. And let them all know what type of snake they were dealin with. He could not trust him. If he would do that to his team, he knew he would do it to him. Because beefing with him would not be good at a time like this. So he had to get rid of him, and fast. Mondo pulled into the Game Room parking lot seeing his leaks car. He parked right next to the Crown Vic on twenty-twos. When he went inside he saw the leak shooting pool by himself. Before Mondo approached the table the leak looked up to see him coming. They dapped each other up.

"Man this shiit crazy!" Tell me about it. I lost my best friend. "Yeah I know." My bad. Well we all supposed to go to this new spot tomorrow. It's across the street in the other Greenhurst. It's off Carmen Street. Once we get settled we are gonna set some shit up to take everything. We are talking about ten bricks, two hundred pounds, fifty X-pills, the whole nine. We split that down the middle, me and you. Mondo loved the way that sounded. "Let's do it. "Be ready in the next couple of days. Skeet, Pary'on and Blackie will be leaving to get this from the plug

Skeet got. Everyone's money is tied into this. This is the re-up for the month for everyone. "Ten-four. Call me. Let's make this one count for Blanks." And he walked off leaving. When he got into the car he pressed the stop button on his recorder. He had all their conversation recorded. This was gonna be the grand finale. Days passed by and Blanks funeral was supposed to be tommorrow. Mondo got all his t-shirts, hats and pants spray painted along with pictures of Blanks and him together. Even one picture at Blanks eleventh birthday party. Mondo was ready to support his best friend. His brother from another mother. He was waiting for the special call. It was one a.m. in the morning when he was sitting in his car sniffing coke listening to Master P. "I miss my homie song. he had the song on repeat. "Sittin in ghetto thinking bout/ all my homies passed away/uuggh//candy painted Cadillac's on tripe gold/that how me and my homies rolled/How could it be/somebody took my boy from me/my best friends gone/and Im so all alone/I really miss my homie/even tho you''ve gone away/I hope your in a better place/ and I hope to see you soon someday....."

Then his phone ranged. If he had to guess he would guess it was Showtime. He answered. "Yo." "Man Come On Now! Ain't nothing but me and Rudy here! Come Now! The shit gonna be too easy!" "I'm coming!" Just like II told you! Come on I don't know how lon they are all gonna be gone! You do remember the layout right?!" "I remember! I'm coming now!" It took Mondo ten minutes to get to the spot. As he entered the neighborhood he slowly crept through the street. Once on Carmen Street, he backed his car into a dead end road. He hit his lights. Mondo eyes got adjusted to the night fast. He slowly opened the door to his car. He got out trying not to make a sound. He need to hear everything. He slowly jogged to the backyard of the Lick's house. he looked around with his AR-15 in both hands. He waited a minute to make his next move. His heart was racing. He slowly opened the backdoor. It made a slight creakin sound but not loud. But Mondo waited tiptoeing towards the washer and dryer room. There was another door and he opened it. It opened with smoothness. He could hear Rudy bragging about their recent re-up, just stood in the kitchen with his back to the wall. He was being extra cautious. He started to breathe in and out slowly. "No Guts, No Glory." He thought to himself. Then he jerked around the corner with his AR-15 leading the way. "DON'T NOBODY MOVE? Rudy and Moose was taken by surprise. "Give it all up now!" Moose playing his roll acted scared. "Please don't shoot! Hold on! Chill!" Rudy moved for his gun. Boom! Mondo shot him in the leg taking off a big chunk of meat. It was not a direct hit to take it all the way off.

Moose told him, "hold up! I'm gonna give you everything! After Moose gave him everything he shot Moose in the face. "FUCK YOU SNAKE!" Then Mondo walked up to Rudy, Rudy crying and begging, "please don't kill me! Ple-please don't!" "Oh I'm not! I know you don't know who I am. But, your homies do! Make sure you give them this. "And Mondo went into his pocket to retrieve the recorder that he's been using to record him and Moose's conversation. "Make sure you give this to Pary'on! The next time me and you meet, I'm do you just like I did that snake ass nigga Moose! Blanks will get his revenge! And he tossed the small recorder at Rudy. He picked up Rudy's gun too. he put it on his as. waistline. Then he picked up the two suitcases pertaining the work. He began running out the house then down the street to his car. He made it to his car and sat there looking down the street at the spot he just came from. He lit a cigarette then cranked his car up to leave. Now he decided to really leave town. He had a few places in South Carolina to hit up with the work he just came up on. Now he had to hire a team of certified hittas, because he was fend to go to war. He knew Pary'on as very liked all through he city. But he was dealing with the whole team now. This one hurts them. Their pockets at least. He did away with their pest control problem. Moose was their least worries. An ememy with money and revenge on their mind became a very strong serious adversary.... "I will avenge Blanks death. Even if I have to go out in cold blood myself. After my dwags funeral, Pary'on you better watch where you be steppin at, because I will be waiting in the dark to snatch your soul nigga..." Mondo said out loud as he drove off smoking a cigarette as tears flowed down his cheeks...

CHAPTER 5

I Live Easy, But I Die Hard

Everyone was at Trident Hospital in the lobby on the secon floor waiting for Rudy to come out, or for the doctor to let them know what was going on. Rudy lost a lot of blood waiting on them to get to the house. Pary'on had the recorder in his hand along with everyone waiting to hear what was on the tape. The lobby was filled with only them. Moose went somewhere else. Dead on Arrival was what the breaking news said. Pary'on hit play on the small recorder. Everyone eyes got big as their ears were glued to the recorder. They listened to the recordin three times before Pary'on heart was crushed. Moose was his dawg, so they thought. Everyone sat in crushing silence at first. Blackie broke the silence. "Man hell no! I can't believe this nigga! "Then everyone started talking at one time. They got so loud until Pary'on looked over at the nurses at the desk peeking at them from time to time. "Yall Shhhh! Them nurses hear us! Let's wait till we hear about Rudy, then we will go to my house for a family meeting." "WE ALREADY KNOW WHAT'S GOING ON! He probably knows where all of us stay! That snake ass bitch gave us all up! We at war! Fuck these nurses! Fuck these niggas! And fuck the police! We took a major lose! Not only in money, but we lost a nigga, who I thought was my friend! And almost lost another one! Man it is war time!" Blackie tried calming Skeet down. Pary'on ran after Skeet. He caught up with him in front of the elevator. "Bruh, I know its war

27

time! But we have to use our resources in these streets! "You can't move that type of weight around in these streets without people talking! That's too much traffic! I'm ready for whatever! But, we cannot move reckless either! Skeet looked at him in his eyes. "Bruh, I feel you. But, I'm going home. This is too much for one nigga. I love you! But I'm going home to my family." "I love you too. Be easy!" Yeah, you too." Skeet got on the elevator. Pary'on walked back into the lobby waiting room with his head down. Everyone was putting their input on the situation. He just sat down thinking. He could not wait to see what "Myspace was saying about everything. Hours later the doctor came out to the lobby. Rudy's mother and girlfriend were there. The doctor approached Rudy's mother. Ma'am your son lost a lot of blood. He almost lost his leg, but we managed. It'll take him a while to get back to walking on two legs again. We are gonna hold him for a week or two. He'll be fine. He is out like a light as of right now. Visiting hours are tomorrow. Right now he need to rest. I will take on two people to sit with him. And thats immediate family only. "Then Rudy's girlfriend stood by his mother, I'll take it. It'll be yall two. Well follow me. Have a good morning to the rest of you. And the doctor dissappeared with Rudy's mother and girlfriend. Everyone left.

Pary'on was looking al over the parking lot. His eyes went to the inside of all the sitting cars parked. He felt he was being watched. Moose fuxked him up. As he hit the alarm to his Beamer, he looked around again as he stood at the driver's door. When he sat down in his seat he reached under the seat to retrive his gun. He placed it on his lap, then put the keys in the ignition. When he was backing out of the parking space, when he turned around to look behind him a scary clown looking face with a pistol in his hand pointed it in his face. All he heard was "Yeah bitch! And the trigger being pulled. Then he jumped up in a warm sweat out of his sleep. Ever since he left the hospital and made it home he's been having dreams of things, and people out to get him. He looked around and no one was in the room with him. He glanced at the clock, and it was ten fifteen in the morning. He got up out his bed. Everything in the dream happened except the last part. Once he placed the pistol on his lap he drove home paranoid. How much did Moose tell Mondo? He knew Mondo through some associates. But he had to find out more. Mondo had to get touch, and soon. Pary'on went to Skeet house from an emergency text from him. Once Pary'on arrived, Skeet was sittin in his living room with an assault rifle in his lap. "Man we about to go to that nigga Blanks funeral. We have to let this nigga Mondo know that his shit real and personal." "Let's go!" Skeet picked up his AK-47 to leave out the kitchen way.

Pary'on followed him. Skeet went to his garage and there was a black Crown Vic with police lights on the driver side. "I got this from a dealership in Columbia. Now I'ma put this stolen license plate on the back. Then we going up in the funeral like we the police. "And they got inside to leave. Once inside, Pary'on notice an obituary with Blanks on the front. He picked it up to look at it while Skeet drove. He then looked at the address of the obituary. They was going to a familiar church. It was big. But. God would have to forgive him. He sure was about to sin. They pulled into the church parking lot and cars were everywhere. Trap niggas were all over the outside of the church. The ones to cool to sit inside. They wore shirts with pictures of Blanks, some were on cell phones walking around pacing and some congregated laughing and dapping up. Some females were around talking to the hustlers flaunting off their assets. When some caught the Crown Vic eye, you could telll they thought that the police was out there. Some even went to shield their faces. "They really think we ball." Skeet said. That was our reasoning for riding in this police car." Pary'on added gripping his nine millimeter. Twenty minutes later the church door opened. "There they go! Skeet pulled down his ski mask so did Pary'on. As soon as the casket was in full site they jumped out guns drawn. The first shot caught people off guard, then shots rained out. Mondo released his hands from the coffin, he then went in his waist band pulling out a Glock 40. He start bussing at Skeet and Pary'on, but all his shots missed their targets. Two of the pallbearers got hit dropping the casket. The top came open then slammed back down as the front of the casket hit the ground hard. They started shooting at some of the hustlers, a few of them had their weapons drawed, but did not get a chance to get a shot off. Skeet kept shooting the hundred round drum. Pary'on jumped inside the car. He crawled across the seat to the drivers side. He cranked the car up. He turned the car to leave out, he leaned over to open the passenger side door. He screame, "Come on Bruh!" Come on!" Skeet jumped inside, and before the passenger side door was closed Pary'on was pulling off once Skeet was inside. "Fuck yeah!" Whoa! That's what I'm talking about! Making a fucking statement!" "Damn Right!" Pary'on added. Pary'on was racing away from the church. He looked in his rearview to see niggas in the middle of the street shooting at them. But they were too far away for the bullets to affect them. You want a war, then bring it PUSSIES!!! Back at the church...It was a bloody mess. Mondo was furious. People were screaming, people were getting into their cars to leave. Mondo could not think straight. The police begin pulling up on the scene. People were screaming what happen to the police officers. Mondo was a wanted man so he had to get out of there somehow. He ran up on this dude on his motorcycle. "Let me hold this homie. "He asked pointing his gun in the man's face. "Damn man! Here! "He said jumping off his own bike. Mondo made it out the church grounds onto the main road. Several ambulances were blaring their lights racing towards the church. Mondo had to leave town. He would pay them back once he got some hittas on his team. He had the money and work to do it too...This was far from over Mr. Pary'on.....

CHAPTER 6

Back 2 Da Future

———————————— ❧ ————————————

Pary'on walked out the pharmacy with his son's prescription. He had to stop by Marie's sister house. Tania was the youngest of her siblings. She had one child she adore so much. She was a single mother, but she got as much help from Pary'on as she needed. What were big brothers for. He pulled up to her spot hours before Marie came home. Before he even got out the car, she showed up to the door holding her miniture french bulldog. They all got out the car. "Hi Aunt Tania! "Hi Nae Nae. i heard Poncho was sick. Yall come inside. "She then walked back inside. Inside she gave Pary'on a hug. "Yall go in the room. Yall staying over here for a while? And the kids went into the room. Pary'on went to Tania's room and laid across the bed. Tania went inside her closet to pull out a fend purse. She was a Marie twin. She just was smaller than Marie and a few shades darker. She still was considered a red girl. She pulled out racks of money. "Thanks Nia. "Tania was his pick up woman and his hold woman. Tania introduced Pary'on to a weed plug when he first got to Ohio. And Pary'on middleman of twenty-five thousand a month without getting his hands dirty. Pary'on had know someone that got the prices very low from California and he got a twenty-five thousand dollar cut off each monhly drop. Tania got the money for him from her friend and he gave her a free two grand for doing that. "No problem." "It'll be a problem if your sister finds out. I told her I am stopping this shit." "Your not doing anything. She should not complain especially the life she is living." "Tell me about it. I have another all white party to throw to hide the real come up. "I don't see her getting mad at you. Your the man any woman would love to marry." "Yeah thats what she wants more than anything. Her bombass wedding." "We'll, your handling that too along with my beautiful face and expertise." "I'm the man for sho." "The best she ever had and will ever need. Lighten up on yourself. We all love you. We won't let her leave you. Fuck if she gets mad if she finds out. She ain't going nowhere, trust me." I run shit, now don't get it twisted! I just don't like my baby mad at me." "No, you just don't want to sleep on the couch with no pussy nigga! And they bust out laughing. "My baby got dat Fyyaaa!" "We all do. Thats why your ass don't want to fuck up." "Your sister love this dick girl! I run shit." "Ok scary! I heard yall goin to Costa Rica next month. The kids going too?" "Yeah, then they coming back while we stay out there for three extra days." "See, this bitch be doing too much. When the family vacation is? "When all the family can be off at the same time." I know thats right Marie. Thirteen years is a long time too. Both of you deserve it." "Can't wait to see my baby face when she sees this new ring I got." "Let me see. And he pulled out his phone. He showed her a few close up pictures of the ring he got designed. "Damn! That ring is so pretty! You got expensive taste! "Thats the walk down ring." "Walk down? Oooohhh! For real! Thats it righr here! She gonna faint when you purpose wih this! Pary'on just smiled his sexy smile. "Get your money and get out my room. "She said leaving out. Come on cutie she called to her puppy. Pary'on laid back pullinfg the blunt from behind his ear. He remembered his meeting with his Cali plug. It was 2007 Summertime after Mondo robbed them and their other plug started acting funny. So Pary'on called his friend from prison's brother. First he got in contact with him to tell his brother he was coming. It took three days for the letter to get to his Mexican friend Carlos. Carlos called him immediately. One night he was Leroy's house when he got the call. "Hello." Pary'on my friend! This is Carlos!" "Hey Carlos." "Hey I called my hermanos. He said he will meet you. I told him I trusted you. So your good. He want you to call him." "Okay." I'ma text you his number. I told you to been get in contact with me if you needed help out there." "Yeah. I know, but I had to make sure I really needed you and your brother." "Well he is gonna make sure your okay. I gave my approval my friend." "I thank you. Twenty-five hundred will be wired Jay pay to you in the morning". "I don't want nothing from you, but to keep the same amount of loyalty you have for me towards my brother." "I sure will, but that money is still coming, look for it.

Gracias harmanos." "Nadada m harmanos." "Call my brother. I have one more year to catch up to yall. Theamos my harmanos." Love you too my brother." Click....Carlos sent Pary'on his brother Guadalupe's number. Pary'on called him. "Hello, may I speak to Guadalupe." "This is me. My brother Carlos told me alot about you. "He said in broken English. Carlos and him both talked the same. "Yeah I just got off the phone with him. So when can we meet up?" "Whenever your ready. I'm sending you my address. Whenever you can make it out here, please come." "I'll come tomorrow if you send the address." "Say no more. He sent the address, and Pary'on got ten X-pills for his ride. He was going to need it. He was going to California. When he arrived in Cali to the address, Guadalupe gave him he place was amazing. It was up in the hills. The road to the nice glass house was loaded with nice palm trees and flowers all the way to the wide circular driveway. There was a nice greek myrhology goddess fountain made of stone in the middle of the driveway. The pond had very nice exotic looking fresh water fish along with several big koi fish. The driveway had a nice yellow drop top ferrari along with a black phantom a burgandy wine Benz G-Wagon truck and a lot of old skool Caprice's 1974 hummers, 64 Chevy Impalas with gold spokes. There was cameras everywhere. Landscapers were all over taking care of the yard trimming the maze walls made of bushes with roses all growing wild throughoout the bushes. It waas very beautiful to see. This was how he wanted to live. He put the car in park then got out. He looked around smiling. The smell was amazing. This was living. Before he got to finish soaking up the scenery, he was called by Guadalupe. He looked at the 5'8 175 pound Mexican that was drapped in a silk Versace button down shirt with cream slacks with black and gold Versace loafers. Medusa's head was in 18k gold in two different spots on the loafers. Guadalupe had a big smile on his face with his hand extended to shake Pary'on's hand. "Guadalupe." Pary'on said as he shook the rich Mexican hand with a firm grip. "Pary'on, I've heard a lot about you my friend, "he said returning his own firm hand shake. "Welcome to my home. I know Carlos can be a bit much. I hope he did not cause you or your people too much problems. He told me how you helped him out with a gambling debt. When some people wanted to stab him over his winnings." "Yeah it was nothing. He is cool with me. I don't like bullies. He was beating them in poker and they wanted to rob Carlos. And I wasn't going for that at all. Guadalupe listened to Pary'on in amazement. He could hear the loyalty in his voice.

Carlos told him he would like Pary'on as soon as he met him. Guadalupe listen to Pary'on for five minutes and he was convinced. Guadalupe stood up from his seat to interrupt Pary'on. "Follow me my friend. "Guadalupe guided Pary'on to his 458 Ferrari. "Get in. "Pary'on got in and they drove off Guadalupe's compound. They rode for a few hours until Guadalupe pulled up to his farm land looking house. "Vin aque Pary'on." "Pary'on knew tha meant come here. Pary'on followed him into the farm looking house. Once inside Pary'on could smell the exotic weed so strong till it was suffocating. They walke through the house and walked into a green house looking at the white clouded glass structure all around from wall to wall, ceiling to ceiling. The sun's radiation passed through the atmosphere so the plants could absorb all of it. The fans and the lights were there so the plants reradiate as radiation of longer wave length that can be absorbed by atmosphere gases so the weed can be harvested healthy and strong. Pary'on looked at the eight foot tall plants that turned into big bushes. The buds were so thick and looked so beautiful. Pary'on estimated one hundred or so weed bushes that was in their harvest stage. He also noticed all different kind of exotic weeds. Then Guadalupe directed him into a different part of the greenhouse where three Mexican men had mountains of exotic weed. Some mountains were four feet tall. They were filling up twenty gallon drums. Then in another room three more Mexicans with mountains of weed were stuffing five gallon paint size buckets of weed. They also labeled the buckets with the names of the weed. Blueberry Dome, Papaya, Purple Allen OG, Purple Punch, Wifi OG, Blue Cheese, Turtle Kush, Smurple, Purple Purple, Girl scout. Irene just caught his eye. Then him and Guadalupe walked into a lab looking room. And Pary'on eyes got big as quarters, when he seen the most cocaine he ever seen in his life. He seen this much on tv when the military or feds advertised an amazing bust. Pary'on almost fainted. Guadalupe noticed his behavior. Are you okay my friend? The look on Pary'on face told it all. "I have NEVER seen this much work at one time. I seen shit like this on tv and read inside books." "Well if you stay loyal this can be all yours my friend. "He told Pary'on smiling. "I'm gonna have to work myself up to this status. This is Tony Montana living. I'm ready to get my feet wet. "Give me a spot to have my friends meet you at. "My house." Pary'on gave Guadalupe his mother's house address." "A wise choice my friend and they left. When they made it back to Guadalupe's house they ate dinner. Pary'on got introduced to Guadalupe's wife and daughter. His daughter Isabella was twenty-two years old. She was 5'6, 150 pounds, thick in all the right placs. She was so beautiful with multiple tattoos. Her black hair came down to her lower back. She was very exotic looking. She smiled at Pary'on displaying a very beautiful smile. Pary'on felt the sexual chemistry. The energy was real thick. They all gave Pary'on a hug then they all sat at the table to eat. The chef bought out some real exquiste food. They had some very expensive champagne poured inside the glasses in front of their plates. The dinner was amazing. Guadalupe got to know Pary'on very well during dinner. "Well Pary'on, Isabella will smoke some weed with you. She has her own smoke room on the other side of the house. I and my wife don't smoke weed so yall enjoy yourselves. I'm going to bed. See you at breakfast." "Okay, Thank you." "Nadada. And Guadalupe left out of the room, Pary'on would be occupying while he would be staying there. Twenty minutes later Isabella knocked at the room door. "Come in." Isabella entered the room with a very short body hugging strapless dress. Her skin was so beautiful. Her tattoos on her shoulders and above her breast stood out. Her ass was so soft, wobbling uncontrollably as the small dress tried to keep her ass cheeks covered with the cotton fabric. She sat down on the bed and Pary'on eyes could not stay focus on her face as he looked down to see that her carmel toe was packed up inside the white thongs she wore. Her pussy was fat. Her inner thighs had a tattoo of multiple flowers. "Are you gonna come smoke exotic with me.?" "Yeah. Lets me use the bathroom, then we can smoke. "Okay, I'll wait right here for you. "Pary'on went to the big bathroom that door was fifteen feet away from the bed inside the room. When Pary'on came out the bathroom, Isabella switched positions on the bed. She was now laying across the bed looking at her phone. Her skirt exposed the bottom half of her fat ass as she laid on her stomach. Her pussy was peeking out the thong. His dick got hard as fuck. She looked at her phone as she reached behind her to pull her skirt down. Without looking behind her, she asked if he was ready. "Yeah lets go." "She got up off the bed too put her flip flops back on her tiny pedicured feet. Pary'on followed behind her trying not to watch her ass movements inside the short skirt. He had to adjust his erection inside his pants. So it could be controlled by his waistline of the pants he wore.

They finally made it to the other side of the mansion. Isabella opened the door to a very nice smoke room. The room had pool tables, arcade machines, ping pong machines, dart throwing boards, small basketball shooting machines with four small basketballs resting inside the net. There was a couch with the cushions that were the size of a regular size bed, bean bags swirl around the bar stools and it even had a movie projection screen to watch movies. Isabella went to the section in the room that had a small door. She opened that door to the size of room walk-in closet and there were jars of weed as if they were in a dispensary. There were nice leather sofas, and other chairs to sit in. Isabella sat down by the weed jars. "Choose which ever ones you want to try. "She did not to tell him twice that's for sure. She gave him the option to smoke out papers, blunts, hookah, bongs, or small pipes. He smoked out a bong first. They were smoking,laughing at each other jokes. Isabella was so close to Pary'on he could feel her body heat. She kissed his neck then moved up to his ears. Pary'on begins responding to her temptations. They begin kissing each other. Then Pry'on thought about being caught by Guadalupe. "Chill". "No you want this just as bad as I do!" She said kissing him again. "Your father will kill me." He won't know!" :My loyalty won't let me. If I met you anywhere else, I would of fuck the shit out of you. "Fuck the shit out me now!" Isabella began grabbing his dick. That was it. She pulled her DD titties out and the nipples were pierced with small bars with balls on the ends. She unbuckled his pants to expose his massive dick. Pary'on begin sucking her nipples as she pulled up and down his dick. She stood up thn grabbed his hand to stand him up. He pulled his pants down to his ankles. She looked him in his eyes then dropped down to her knees. She began sucking his dick fast but seductively. As she sucked his dick she was playing in her own pussy. She got up off her knees and bent over in front of Pary'on. Her fat juicy ass was in front of him as she kneeled in the small couch. Pary'on pulled her thong to the side as entered into her warm moist pussy. He begin going uncontrollably inside her vagina walls. "Ooohh, shit papi!!! Fuck yeah! Fuck Me! Yesss! Yes zaddy!" Isabella moaned out loud. Pary'on beat it up. Then Isabella wanted to ride him. She pushed him down on the couch.She looked down at his dick then she pulled her small skirt over her ass cheeks. She pulled her thong off then straddled him. She begin riding his dick slow. She had to stuff her own thongs in her mouth because she was making too much noise. She began nutting all over his dick. Then her mama's voice could be heard calling her name in her broken English language. They both had the look of shock on their faces. She jumped off Pary'on then pulled her skirt down and pulled the skirt over her DD breast. Once she did that she left Pary'on in the room as she darted out to her mother. "Yes ma'am! Mrs. Maria smiled when she saw her daughter. "Is everything ok with Pary'on? Where is he?" "Oh yeah we just was smoking. I left him inside the weed chambers because I heard your voice." I have to ask him something. "And her mother begin walking towards the room. She entered the room to see Pary'on fully dressed with his back to the door looking at the jars of weed. "Pary'on." "Pary'on turned around to Mrs.Maria smiling face. "Yes ma'am."

What do you want for breakfast? I'm asking because the chef has a schedule. And at nine o'clock breakfast will be bought to the table. We eat breakfast on the outside deck with the view over the city from the mountain tops. "Anything will be good for me. I will defintely enjoy whatever. "Okay." We always cater to our guest. "Thank you. But whatever everyone else is having will be good for me. "Okay Gwenos nochos." "Gwenos nochos." And she left. Isabella and Pary'on looked at each other like that was a close call. Once ther were alone again Isabella spoke up first. "I guess I'll be going to bed too. Next time will be a full sex session. I'll settle for that for now. Next time I will make sure we will finish. "She kissed Pary'on on the cheek then walked out. Pary'on shook his head as Isabella picked up her thongs off the floor then left out. Pary'on tried more weed before he made his way to the guest bedroom he was occuping. Minutes later he fell asleep. The next morning he was half assleep with his eyes still closed he smelled a very sweet exotic perfume smell so close to his nose he had to open his eyes. Isabella was standing so close to him that all he could see when he opened his eyelids, was her fat camel toe packed up inside her silk Gucci boy shorts. "Time for breakfast papi. "She bent down and planted a wet kiss on his forehead. "Gwenos Dias papi trulo. "And she walked off leaving Pary'on dick hard. He watched her fat soft ass cheeks jiggle from every strut she took. When she left out the room, Pary'on shook his heas then screamed out, "FUCK!" He got up to go to the bathroom to get him ready for breakfast. Ten minutes later Pary'on was walking out to the top deck table outside. "Gwenos Dias Pary'on! Guadalupe and his wife called out to Pary'on. "Gwenos Dias!" he said back with a smile. He sat by Isabella. It was actually the closest empty chair. As they enjoyed breakfast, Isabella was playing under the table. He trie to keep his composure in front of Guadalupe. She stroked his dick on top of his demin monkey shorts. After breakfast, fresh fruit was bought to the table by the chefs. Guadalupe fired up a cigar; the sweet smell of the tobacco could have still been smelled in the morning breeze air. "Everything will be waiting for you my friend as soon as you get home. Here is a cell phone only for business, untraceable. You don't call any other number but the numbers that are programmed. Any other number and it puts the whole operation at risk. Then I'm not responsible for anythin that happens to you after that. Let's make millions. "Then he handed Pary'on the cell phone. "There is nothing else to talk about at this moment. You should get going!

You have a lot of work to do my friend, I'll have my eyes on you. You don't have to contact me unless there is a problem or your are finish. Any problems please just give us a name and it'll be our problem. I'm sure you know how to handle yourself, but I'll be by your side if you need me my friend. I have to go now. We will do this again soon. Idos Amigo." Idos Guadalupe. Trust me I'm down for life. Let's get it. "They shook hands and Pary'on was on his way. He could not wait to get back to South Carolina. Pary'on ride back was easy. When he was getting off the Don Holt Bridge to enter in the country he noticed a white van with tinted windows riding close behind him and was taking every turn he was turning. He clutched on his pistol then pulled into a gas station. As he looked in his mirror the van followed him. He then drove around the gas station parking lot trying to see the driver of the van. He parked at the number 5 gas pump and then notice the van parked right behind him. "Man what the fuck? If yall want these problems then so be it. Let's do this in broad day light then. Pary'on thought out loud. He jumped out the car with his Jordan book bag in hand. His other hand was inside the book bag with his hand wrappe around his Glock 22. As he approached the van the window on the driver's side began rolling down. He was surprised to see two very light complexion Mexican's in the drivers and passenger seat. They began smiling at him, and speaking Spanish very fast. All he could make out was Guadalupe's name that was said. And they flashed the same kind of cell phone Guadalupe gave him. He put two and two together fast. He ran back to his car. And as he drove off they drove off too. When they pulled to his mother's ten acre yard he drove to the side of the land that was blocked off by the thick woods. When he knew everything was good, he waved to the Mexicans to get out the van. The two short workers dressing looking amigos jumped out ot the van. They went to he back door of the van to open the doors. And three other Mexicans with assault rifles jumped out the back. Pary'on shook his head in surprise. When he looked in the back of the van, his eyes got big from seeing all the packages of blocked saran wrapped drugs. Only one of the five Mexicans spoke English. "The green wrappings are marijuana. The other wrappings are cocaine. "He said in a broken English speech. As the three Mexicans unloaded the van the other two stood watch holding on to their assualt rifles. Pary'on watched the Mexicans unload the van. He could not believe how much work he had. His stomach begin turning. He suddenly had to take a shit. I'll be back my friends. Give me five minutes. "I'm going in the house right quick." The Mexicans that spoke both English and Spanish translated what Pary'on had said to the other four. Pary'on heart was beating hard. He hoped no one come home until he could find out what to do next. He ran into the house straight to the bathroom. After he finished using the bathroom he washed his hands then looked at his reflection in the mirror. He smiled a big cheesy grin. "I'm Breaded now bitches! Let's do this! "Then he returned back outside. When he walked back to the unload spot all of them was smoking cigarettes watching out for any approaching threat. Are you good my friend?" The English speaking Mexican asked. "Yes." "Can we leave now?" "Si". He spoke to his compardes and they got inside the van and left. Pary'on scratching his head. There was twenty-five green blocks and ten white blocks. Pary'on picked up one of the green blocks. Each blocks was the size of a large microwave inside the box. Pary'on ran back inside his mother's house and grabbed her human body digital scale from her bathroom. He ran back outside. He placed one of the blocks on the scale. The scale read thirty pounds. So he figured it was twenty-five pounds of weed in each block and five pounds of plastic wrap with the petroleum jelly and instant coffee mix to block off the smell.

Pary'on had to hide this much work. He called Skeet. "Where are you at? "At my baby mama's house." "Bruh!" Come to my mama house ASAP! And bring your Tahoe Now!" Skeet heard the emergency in Pary'ons voice. Come by myself?" "Hell yeah!" Don't even tell nobody where you going!" Alright. I'm coming now!" Click...By the time Skeet got out ro the country Pary'on done moved the blocks to his single car garage he had for his 69 Chevelle. Pary'on was smoking a blunt when Skeet pulled his Tahoe around the side of the house. Skeet saw Pary'on pacing, He placed his Tahoe in park leaving the truck running as he jumped out running up to Pary'on. "What's up bruh?" Pary'on walked up to the wooden one car garage and opened the two heavy wooden doors. Skeet eyes popped out his head. "What the fuck!! That's work?!! Pary'on smiled shaking his head yes. Skeet ran up to Pary'on hugging and picking him up. Pary'on hugged him back. "Boy we on!" "Skeet slapped Pary'on hand over and over until they finally dapped each other up embracing each other. "I don't even wanna know right now my nigga! Lets get rid of this shit!" "Fosho!" Pary'on pulled out a box cutter and sliced open the white wrapping first. A strong aroma od a mixture of gasoline, ammonia or either gas. The cocaine was stink. After Pary'on got most of the wrap off the block his whole hand was greasy and brown from the instant coffee. The box cutter kept slipping out his hand, so he looked around the yard to find some old dirty towels used to dry the car off that was hard dried. He begin cleaning his hands. "How much coke is this? "Skeet asked looking at the most coke at one time he ever seen face to face. "I don't know. They just dropped it off." "They." And Pary'on explained what was on. "Man, man, man! Shit yea! And once they got the coke package cleaned up they put it on the picnic table. They did the same thin o the other coke pack. And five weed packs. Pary'on told everyone to go to the new spot. hey put all the clean packages inside Skeet's Tahoe. Pary'on and Skeet went to the dollar store to buy a padlock for the single car garage. They locked the doors up then left to go to the spot. After a few months, the city knew that the click was back on top and even better than ever. They had the city on smash and surrounding areas. Now Pary'on had the women chasing him for real, But he had one particular woman name Gina all over him. She use to be a high profile stripper that knew all the big time hustlers from South Carolina, parts of Flordia and other states. She started serving major weed and ecstacy pills all over. So Pary'on became her new supplier on the weed. Plus they had the friends with benefits type of relationship that many speculated, but did not know for sure if they were fucking!

But someone had a close eye on the two and she was furious every time she saw them two together. Isabella was watching in her 2008 Impala as Gina got out her X5 BMW Jeep going into Pary'on's house. Isabella spoke out loud in rage. "I'm tired of your shit bitch, I'm making that call. "It was 2 a.m. and Isabella was acting like a jealous ex. She grabbed her phone and speed dialed a number. "Hola." She has to go. I'm at the casa right now. Vena qui." Si cheeka. "Click...Isabella watched Pary'on play with this bitch too long. Gina was 5'3 about 140 pounds, thicker than a snicker model straight out a stunning photo shoot. She mixed Black, white and Indonesian. Isabella hate her lonf silk looking hair. She watched Gina deliver much money to Pary'on. But she hated her even more once she seen her stay the night with Pary'on after dinner. Isabella had on a long purple trench coat with matching color monolo blanik boots. She looked sexy every time she came to South Carolina to spy on Pary'on. Her father did not know she was obessed over Pary'on. It was her first time being with a black man. And Pary'on acts as if she meant nothing to him. And she had to let him know that she was not the one. She was the head of a major cartel and he must know she is part of the reason he is eating. When she got the call she has been waiting on, Qui pasa." We are turning on the street." Pull up in the yard. "Click...Isabella placed her Glock 30 inside her trench coat pocket then cranked up the car. She saw the car lights of her back up coming down the street. They pulled up in the yard and existed the Ford Excursion. One ran up to the front door with a small black bag the size of a crown royal bag. He put some untensils in his hand, then placed them inside the door's key hole. In seconds the door was open. They move like ninjas through the house. They got to

Pary'on's room and entered inside. They did not turn on the lights until they disarmed Pary'on. His pistol was on the table next to him. Then Isabella turned the lights on inside the room, the fifteen muscle group Isabella called on to apprehend both Gina and Pary'on. Isabella stood in front of the king-size bed looking at the incident unfolded, when Pary'on eyes locked on Isabella. "Take the girl out and leave me alone with Pary'on." They did as their boss said. When Gina was being escorted by the four Mexicans with tattoos all over their faces holding her, stopped in front of Isabella. Then Isabella focused her full attention on Giina. Looking Gina in her face she said, "this type of shit happens to you when you're fucking another woman's prize winner. The Business part was bothering first. But once you started fucking him then that is where you fucked up. Maybe we could have fucked him together. But you must not mess with another woman's property. Take her to the chambers. I'll be there when I get there. Don't kill her until i get there. "After the words, don't kill her came out of Isabella's mouth, Pary'on jumped up out of the bed but stopped dead in his tracks when he was face to face with eight guns. As Isabella pointed her Glock 30 at his head she said, "Please don't make me kill your sexy ass.

Sit down on the bed. Now!" As Pary'on sat down all the pistols followed him. Some had red dots all over his head and chest area. "Exit the premises everyone! And in seconds the house was empty accept for Isabella and Pary'on. She smiled at him as she pointed her Glock 30 towards his head. She looked at his naked body up and down. She got wet between her legs. She lowered her gun placing it on the dresser next to her. She then pulled the belt unloose from the loosely knot that held her trench coat closed. Her coat came open exposing her barley naked body in purple lace matching bra and thong. She grabbed her pistol then walked over to Pary'on. She pointed the gun to his head and then pushed him back on the bed. She then fell to her knees. She placed the tip of the glock under his balls. Then she began sucking his dick. He was between hard and soft. She began sucking his dick so good he tried not to get hard with a glock to his nuts. But she sucked his dick so good, a porn star would be proud of her performance. When his dick got all the way hard she pulled her panties to the side, then straddled him. As she got onto his massive dick going in and out of her soaked pussy she lowered her pistol and let it fall to the bed. She began riding him wildely. Pary'on tried so hard not to enjoy this, but he could not help himself. He gained control of the situation and he began fucking the shit out of Isabella. He then started hitting her from the back. He picked up the Glock 30 then as he was stroking her pussy he pointed the gun toward her head he fucked her even harder then got his nut. After he nutted all over Isabella's ass he kept the gun pointed at her. She was still in the moment of bliss. She reached for her glock then when she realizes that it was not in her grasps so she turned over to Pary'on pointing the glock at her. "What are you gonna do? If you kill me, my father will kill your mother, brothers, sisters and their kids in your face. All of them will be raped in your face then killed. Even Marie out there in Ohio. She seen his face drained of life as she spoke the truth to him. She began rubbing her clit in his face as she begin speeding up, her eyes rolled in the back of her head as she begin cumming all over her fingers. Pary'on could not believe what was happening. "I don't play Pary'on." Put that gun down and go get my money out them streets!" Isabella got up off the bed then walked up to Pary'on then grabbed her gun. Pary'on kept a firm grip on i. "How do I know you won't kill me anyway?" Isabella smiled slyly. "Because I actually like you. Now don't make me start disliking you. Watch how your moving when your handling the cartels money. Now as for your little bitch don't fuck her again or I will kill her myself until the next time my love. "Isabella pulled the gun from Pary'on grasp softly, grabbed her trench coat then left. Without looking back she said, your next package is on the way. I'll get in contact with you for the money before I leave town. My services are needed in other states down south. Chow! Pary'on sat on the bed in pure shock and disgust. He did not want to talk to Guadalupe about Isabella. But he had to somewhat check her and put her in her place. So he thought long and hard about his next move. And as he smoked on a blunt a lightbulb went off in his head. He grabbed his phone then started texting Isabella:

Cum 2 this address tonight alone. 150 Carlories Dr.

We have to talk. 7:48 a.m. sent

She text back ten minutes later

I sure will sweetheart. 7:58 a.m.

Pary'on called Gina's phone and it went to the answer machine. He got himself together then did his rounds to get his money out of the streets. He first pulled up to Chill &Thugga spot in the creek. Goose Creek was a diamond mine for cash. When Pary'on pulled up in the Devon forest neighborhood, he notices all the $175,000 to $400,000 dollar homes had all kinds of cars and women walking with baby strollers. Some jogging, laying out in the yard soaking up the wonderful morning heat. Some was grabbing their morning paper out their driveway or yard. It was almost 10:45 a.m. and Pary'on knew Chill & Thugga would be ready for him. Pary'on was about to pullin the driveway of their two story home but the driveway was full up. The garage was up and Pary'on saw "Chill's 2008 AMG Benz on 22 inch assanti rims on one side then Thugga's G-Wagon Benz on the other side. Then Chill's 1977 Chevelle on 26 inch rims stood out in the bright sun with candy apple red paint job. And a Dodge Ram 3500 that Thugga drove all the time. The driver's door was open. Then as Pary'on parked halfway on the grass he notice a exotic looking thick short carmel complexion female jumping out the truck. She had on a short silk robe that barley covered her fat ass. Her furry pink Chanel slippers exposed her fresh pretty pedicured toes. She starred at Pary'on until he got out the car. When Pary'on approached her, she said, "Good morning" exposing a full set of pretty teeth. "Damn sure is. Chill & Thugga inside!" They are". "Who are you?" "Pary'on." Her facial expression said it all. She was now face to face with the man she heard so much about throughout the streets, beauty salons, clubs, just about everywhere she went. She smiles a sly grin. "I'm Erica." "Fa sho. Let's go inside. "Pary'on had three duffle bags with him one in each hand by the small handles and the other on over his right shoulder. As he walked behind Erica he could not help but to see her ass. Shaking uncontrollably with every step. And she smelled good. Once they walked through the garage, they entered inside the house. Pary'on kept walking till he walked inside the living room where Chill & Thugga was surrounded wih money and three money counting machines on the glass table. "What's up muthafuckas? Chill jumped up first to dap Pary'on up. "Just the man I need to see." "I'm right on time. "Pary'on passed the duffle bags to Chill. Then he dapped and embraced him and Thugga.Chill had money piled up all over the couch, table and on the floor by his feet. There were shoe boxes full of knot of money, plastic Wal-Mart bags full of money, designer book bags full of cash as well. Thugga had money sprawled out over the Persian rug. They both was blowing on big blunts as they were trying to get money right. Pary'on slid the piles of money on the floor as he plopped down on the end of the couch. He grabbed an unusual looking assault rifle Chill had leaning against the couch cushion. "What the fuck!" Pary'on face screwed up looking at the rare choppa. "That is my baby right there! Chill said smiling showing off his permanent gold teeth smile. Pary'on grabbed the Playstation 3 controller off the table to unpause the NBA 2K game they were playing that was left unattended on the 82 inch wall based Plasma TV. Then the aroma hit the house mixing with the weed smoke of a wonderfully cooked breakfast. Minutes later a light-skinned black mixed Hawaiian slim thick woman came with a big plate full of food walked up to Chill handing him the plate. She looked at Pary'on and smiled a welcoming smile. "Good morning, are you staying for breakfast?" "Shit yeah!" Then Chill intervened. "This my people Pary'on. He a good nigga. Give that man some of that good pussy." "Okay daddy. You want me to fuck him now, or on our own time?" "Whenever my dawg ready. Right now go fix him something to eat." "Okay." Then she walked into the kitchen. This was normal for three dawgass niggas that never put hoes first, Twenty minutes later Erica came from upstairs fully dressed. She stood in front of Thugga who was still counting money. I'ma about to go to class. Can I get a few dollars for lunch?" Thugga gave her thirty dollars in ones. She did not complain one bit. Her friend Yalesha finishing getting ready to go back to Charleston Southern University with Erica. Yalesha walked to Pary'on and asked for his phone number. She sent him a text message then stored his name and number in her contacts. "I guess we'll get up later or something. I'll hit you up after my last class. I'm off tonight so whatever's clever." "Fa sho! Holla at me when your finishing handling all your business." "Will do. Bye yall! And the ladies left out. After two hours, Chill and Thugga finish couning all the money. Chill started pulling out the bricks of coke and pounds of weed, fifteen bricks and fifty pounds. Then all three of them started repacking the duffle bag up with the money. After the bags were stuffed they chopped it up for a while, then Pary'on left to go to the next spot. Before he left Chill had a lot of his blood homies come pick up the several packs. He watched them cut four of the bricks to make extra profit which was fine by him. The coke he was giving them could stand to be hit quite a few more times and still be considered stupid clean. Chill and Thugga still had money on the table. All profit. "See yall in two weeks. "And Pary'on left out the house. His next few stops only paid him $25,000. He had to collect from his little up and coming hustlers he knew was loyal. As the day was unfolding he had to get Skeet's part of the money so he could go meet Isabella. After he loaded the drop off car to switch with Isabella he called her. She picked up on the second ring. "Yes baby." "Meet me at the spot." "Okay." Little did Pary'on know she was already waiting on him.

As the charger Pary'on was driving pulled up to the spot, he did not notice Isabella's charger in the woods. She watched him for five minutes until her phone rang. "Yes sweetheart." "I'm at the spot." "So am I. "Then Isabella flashed the headlights on the charger. She then drove out the woods and parked next to Pary'on's charger. "She jumped out the car then jumped in the passenger side of Pary'on's charger. "What did you come up with Pary'on?" Check this Isabella. I don't want to fuck with you in no type of way period. You are a very beautiful woman, but I'm about business. Your father will kill me if he finds out. You was raised on loyalty. I don't feel loyal fucking my plugs daughter. Even Carlos would feel some type of way about this. You are out of pocket this morning. I'm not scared to go to war with your father's team at all. I have some niggas ready to go to war with anybody with me. But, I respect your mother and father enough not to kill their only child. I was about to kill you this morning. Don't ever pull a gun on me again and don't do me. Because I'm not gonna take it lightly. I am gonna stand firm as a man ten toes down before I allow my nuts to be tested. Now let's make this exchange. I have money to get. "And he jumped out the car leaving her sitting in the passenger seat. He jumped in the driver's side of the empty charger not even looking Isabella's way. Isabella could not say anything. Pary'on made his understanding understood. She got out the car then walke over to the driver's side of the Charger Pary'on was sitting in. She open the door and Pary'on held his hand out to receive the car keys without looking her way. Isabella dropped the car keys in Pary'on's hand then walked off humble. She respected Pary'on for checking her the way he did. And she was right. It was not loyal. So once he got the keys he rode off leaving Isabella behind him.

CHAPTER 7

Present Time

───────────────⁕───────────────

After a day of collecting Pary'on got a call from an old friend ISABELLA! "Yo." "Quispasa Pary'on?" "Ain't shit, whats the deal? My uncle Carlos was murdered in cold blood. "Pary'on heart fell to the floor. "Wha?" "Yeah. And my father is still recovering fom that bad stroke. He is still on bed rest. We don't want to tell him in the condition he is in. But I need your help. Since daddy has been going through his illness other rival cartels have been trying to take our whole family's power out. And with Uncle Carlos now gone that put another gap in our caste wall. You have been my father's and uncle's closes allies, plus you know the in's and out's of the operation. A lot of people respect you in these streets of the United States. We need your help, or we all will be dead in a few years. They would not expect a bunch of black people to be ready to go to war over my family's empire. Please step in with us and reach out to some of your friends for us. We will supply them with all the artillery they need. And we will flood yall streets with the best Cocaine, Heroin, Ice and marijuana. Just let us know when and where. Pary'on was still mind boggled by all of this. He was retired out of the game. He just dibbled and dabbed here and there doe the sport. Life was great for him and his family. And he owed it all to Carlos and Guadalupe. "Let me get something in perspective. I'll call you back on this number. I have to think and breathe for a minute. It won't be long. I'll call you." "Please don't turn your back on my family. We never turned our backs on you and yours. I'm texing you the address to the new meet up spot. Come with your heart filled of loyalty and hatred for our enemy. I expect to see you face to face within a few days. If not then you have added on to the problem and that won't be tolerated. Hopefully I'll see you. Loyalty is what we are made of. The heart ain't shit without loyalty. You can survive alone on loyalty. Let's see where yours lie," and she hung up. Seconds later Pary'on phone chimed letting him know he got a text message. He looked to see the address out in EL Paso, Texas. Pary'on could not believe the call he just reeived. Minutes later Marie came home from work. The kids could have been heard screaming. "Mommy!" Pary'on heard her ask the kids, "where is your Daddy?" And he heard Nae Nae say, in the room. "Marie made her way up the spiral wooden stairs. When she got in the room Pary'on was laid across their big king size canopy wooden bed on his back fully clothed. Marie said, "What's up Daddy?" in a cheerful voice as she used the three steps to get on top of their tall bed. She crawled across the bed and collapse on top of Pary'on kissing his lips. She seen the emptiness on his face. She knew something was wrong. "Whats wrong honey bun? "She asked wiping his face gently. Carlos just got gun down by a rival Cartel. And I got a call for me to get to Texas within the next couple of days." For the funeral right?" He knew right then and there this conversation was about to turn left. When he did not answer her right away. She knew what that call was about. "No!No!HELL NO!NO BABY! I work too hard for this relationship to get it back and then yanked from me by the streets AGAIN! I put up with that shit for ten years! Nope I will not do it again! Fuck No! Your never gonna be out of debt to them! You have two kids for Christ sake Pary'on!" And you think I don't know that? If it was not for me meeting Carlos, we would not be living in this house we are in or driving the cars we drive or our bank accounts would not be climbing the way it is from our businesses." "MAN FUCK ALL OF THIS SHIT! I work enough to live on a nice ball as budget! You don't need any of this! I got us! We can go broke and I am not leaving! I don't care about any of this! I care about our family baby!" Then her voice started to crack up. "It's either them or Us! And she broke down crying. She jumped off the bed and ran out the room slamming the door behind her. Pary'on just laid on the bed and blew out air shaking his head. He was fine living the life he was living. But he had to show his face in Texas. Carlos was his friend. He did not know if he wanted to gt back into the lifstyle that way for Carlos. Because he had an enemy far greater from his lsat enemy Mondo. He had to go against a Cartel. And it is hard beefing with an enemy with that kind of leverage in the streets and that kind of money and drugs.

He had a big decision to make. And he had to make it fast. Knowing Isabella she would look at his not helping as disrespect. Then she would bring the wrath to his door step. But he does owe this girl and kids his life. He would not lose his life being the family man he is now for his family. Only if someone brought the drama to them. But, he knew he had a greater chance losing his life leaving them alone going to help out Isabella. He could not do it. He loved Marie too much. So he went to let her know. When he went out toi let her know he notice the house was quiet. "Marie! Baby! Kids! Where yall at?! He yelled rom the top of the stairs. He jogged down stairs to an empty house. He ran outside to their driveway and all the cars were there except Marie's very first car, a 2007 Honda Accord. It was the car she got for graduation. Pary'on hooked it up with 22 inch rims and a paint job. When he first met her face to face. He called her. No answer. He called her five times and she did not answer. He knew it was needless to keep trying. Then he went back in the house shakin his head pacing. An hour went by and he heard his phone text message ding. It was from Marie:

> I can't do it anymore. We are not married. That's the life you choose. I sacrificed 10 years of my life for you. All the long nights alone, the cheating the worrying. I'm done! Leave us alone, and go live your life. Because once you go to that funeral, your gonna want revenge for your friends death! You can't sacrifice for us when we need you the most! Just be careful!! We love you more than you us! The greatest you'll ever have! Was your 1st Lady! Don't text back either! Received 8:38 p.m.

Pary'on grabbed a cigarillo to bust down. He smoked back to back until he drops to sleep. Once he woke up he did not wake up to his kids screaming, or the smell of his wifey cookin. He dragged himseld off the bed stressing. He texted Marie ten text messages. And she only sent one to him. And he received it: 7:20 a.m. He knew Marie was dropping the kids off because she had to be to work at 8 o'clock. And when he opened it his heart skipped a few beats:

> Please go handle your business and leave us the "F" alone! My family know not to give my kids to you! You lost privilege! You better hope you don't end up like Carlos! Hopefully one day you'll grow up! And hope another man won't be raising your kids and they call him DADDY! Hopefully you'll grow out all

that street life before that that happens. I'm focus on me and my kid's future. Because if it's up to you. (IDK). Dont chase us! Go do what you figure you do best Asshole!! SMH! Received 7:20 a.m.

Pary'on stayed in bed smoking blunt after blunt for days trying to figure out what his next move was. He never wanted things to turn out the way they were now with Marie. But like she said, "She put up with my shit for ten years." I never turned my back on my friends either. Then Pary'on put his phone on the Bluetooth speaker connection then put it on youtube as he went to take a shower. As he showered and once he finished he just stood under the hot water thinking and hoping to let his sorrows go down the drain as the water did. Then one of his favorite songs started playing byYung Dolph, and then he began rapping the song. "keep it real with ya dawg no matter what Preach/same bitch ya fuckin she'll set ya up/(preach)

out here in dez streets/it ain't no such thing is luv/da only thing I trust is dez pistols and dez slugs/(preach). "Keep it real wit ya dawg no matter wat ya doing. NO MATTER WAT!" Pary'on repeated over and over. He knew he had to show up for Carlos. It was only right. So he rushed to get dress and jumped in his Benz G-Wagon and put the cordanents to EL Paso, Texas. It took Pary'on two days to get to the address Isabella sent him. When he pulled up to the Mansion's gate it opened after a minute of him sitting waiting. It was nighttime as he was driving up the long driveway towards the house. As he was looking around the premises he notice shadowy figures all over the place with inferred beams pointing towards him. Was this a setup, or one of Isabella sick ass games again. He sure was about to find out. He jumped out the G-Wagon after he parked close to the twenty foot double front door entrance to the mini castle. And he was rushed by fifteen Mexican soliders with machine guns and assault rifles. He raised his hands in the air not being stupid. They patted him down for any type of weapons. Once his Glock 40 was taken from him he really felt helpless, "Vena qui" was all that was said to him and he did as he was told. He followed them into the house. They led him into a room with a sixteen foot long mahogany and oak wood table. And to his surprise Isabella was sitting at the head of the table along with some powerful looking men. Some in suits, and some dress down like cowboys hats. But, everyone was Spanish. "It's very nice you can finally join us Pary'on. "Isabella spoke up. Pary'on sat down at the empty seat at the head of the long round table. Isabella would of spazz out if it was anybody else sitting in her father's seat, But she had faith in Pary'on's ability to be the activating boss since her fathwr was down and Carlos was dead. Isabella starte speaking in Spanish to everyone about Pary'on. A couple of the members knew Pary'on, but eighty percent did not know him. "This is Pary'on. He is a very strong loyal friend of my uncle Carlos and my father down south distributor. They both have much faith in him. Plus, he has muscle out there where he is and we need a strong loyal knight on this chess table. "Pary'on could feel that he was the topic of conversation. Everyone began looking at Pary'on. They nodded at Pary'on in approval. The meeting lasted another hour. Then Isabella told Pary'on to follow her. She began bringing him up to speed about the meeting due to she was speaking Spanish. They went to her office to talk. She could not help herself, but to lust off the sexy man in front of her. He was dressed in all black. He had on Versace silk shirt sleeve button down, satin slacks with black suede Versace loafers. His gold iced out Rolex, with 22 carat gold Gucci link necklace and bracelet and gold rings with three carat diamond earrings stood out with black his Versace outfit. His freshly cut hair with his deep waves it made. Isabella wet. She really loved this man in front of her. But he belonged to Marie. She sat at her desk then fired up a stuffed cigar. She passed it to Pary'on who was sitting halfway off the big wooden desk. "How is your father coming along?" She sighed, before answering him. "He is the one who summoned you. He wants me to bring you to him once you got here. "Where is he?" We have an underground room built under the mansion. Would you like to see him now?" Sure! It's been a long time. "Okay." They both exited the office to an elevator. Once the door was open they were met by multiple assault rifles. "We brought him down here after threats of his assignation. "They walked past everyone to a vault like small door, Isabella showed Pary'on how to open the door along with the combination. Once Pary'on saw Mrs. Maria by Guadalupe's bedside. When Pary'on saw Mrs. Maria, she still had her beautiful looks but she was just aging. He must say she was aging well. When she saw Pary'on a smile came across her face then she started crying once she got up and ran to him embracing him. "Senor Pary'on, como estea?" "I'm okay Mrs. Maria. You still look so beautiful. Guadalupe is a very special lucky man." "I'm so glad you're here. He wanted to see you. "Mrs. Maria ran to her husband's side. "Papi, papi, look who is here! Sensor Pary'on! "She gently rubbed her husband cheek. Guadalupe's face was wrinkling a little. He looked his age for sure from the last time.

Pary'on seen him since he left from the states to go back to Mexico. Guadalupe woke up finally. He barley opened his eyes. But, his voice was crisp but soft. "Pary'on!" Mr. Hemanos

Com estes?" I'm here my friend. What do you need me to do? Then Guadalupe sat up, then Mrs. Maria fixed his pillows behind him then used the remote to move the back up for Guadalupe. Guadalupe extended his hand for Pary'on to shake it. Pary'on notice an AK-47 by his bedside and a nine millimetet pistol next to his right leg. Pary'on smiled at his mentor's heart. "Yall ladies let me have a bit alone time with Pary'on." And isabella and her mother left out. Mrs. Maria kissed her gold rosary beads then kissed Pary'on cheek before leaving.Once the door was closed Guadalupe put the chair right next to his bed next to the AK-47. Pary'on sat down. "Let's get down to business. You have been in this family for twelve and we all trust you. Do you remember Cruz? Pary'on's face frowned and looking up trying to remember. Then he remembered. "Your Puerto Rican friend we went to see in New York right?" That's him. We don't communicate by phone. Do you remember where he lives or his restuarant? I never took nobody else there but Carlos." "I remember where the restuarant is and the amazing food" "Well I'ma sneak out with you tonight. We need to go therw." "No I'll go there for you." "See, I mus go with you. I need his arms and crew! I got a visit from a family member in Mexico and they is a leak from the other side. They told me that Carlo was first then me. They don't break promises. So we must go as soon as possible." How are we gonna do that? "Help me to my chair. "Pary'on helped him out into the electric wheelchair. And they went to the entrance to the room. Guadalupe begins speaking Spanish to the guards standing outside the door. And just like that two of them exscorted him and Pay'on on the elevator. They came out into the mansion. The two guards swept the area before Guadalupe exited the elevator. They went staight outside to Pary'on's G-Wagon. Guadalupe instructed the two guards to get in the back seat. And they drove off. After about an hour into their escape Pary'on's phone started ringing. He looked at the caller ID of the bluetooth on the twelve inch screen to see it was Isabella. "That's your daughter Guadalupe." "Answer it!." "Pary'on pressed the button on the steering wheel to answer the call. And Isabella blasted off. "I'm gonna cut your balls off and feed them to that red bitch Marie if you don't bring my father back here now!" Then Guadalupe begin speaking Spanish to her. They both went back-n-fourth for a while until Guadalupe told Pary'on to hang up. The Car went into complete silence the whole ride until Guadalupe was hungry and had to use the bathroom. Then on I-95 as they got closer to New York, Pary'on could see the Statue of Liberty. Pary'on did not know the proper directions to the restaurant. But he damn sure remembered the name of it. So he typed the name inside his GPS and it took him straight to Spanish Harlem. Once they got in front of the restaurant it was just like Pary'on remembered. Pary'on jumped out then ran inside to find Cruz, Once inside the restaurant it was somewhat dry. Pary'on walked to the back where he first got escorted to Cruz's office. Then the workers started screaming at him in Spanish and English. But he ignored all of them. He reahed Cruz's office and opened the door. Before he could say anything multiple guns was pointing to his head. Then he was swept off his feet then slammed to the ground. Cruz jumped from behind the desk with a very sharp shiny machete. "Flip him over!" Three very strong Puerto Rican men pulled Pary'on up to his feet. Cruz was a very short Puerto Rican, older looking man with a mouth full of plarinum open faced teeth. His salt-n-peppa hair was in a ponytail that stopped in the middle of his back. He pointed the machete so close to Pary'on's neck, if he moved to quick his neck would be bleeding. "Who are you and what are you doing in my office?" I'm here for Guadalupe! He is sick and needs your help!' At the sound of Guadalupe, Cruz had them release Pary'on. "What is this your talking about?" He is outside in my G-Wagon! He is very sick! I came here with him years ago! Like ten years ago! "Cruz looked closer at Pary'on. Then his memory startsd coming back to him. He closed in quickly for a hug. "I'm sorry my friend! Take me to Guadalupe Now!" And they rushed out to the G-Wagon. Pary'on opened the passenger door so Cruz could see Guadalupe. Cruz's heart felt sorry for his best friend. "Lupe what happen my brother? Talk to me Cruz grabbed Guadalupe cheeks as he spoke him. "We will talk, but not here. I"m calling a car for the both of us. And my doctor will be at the Casa when we get there. Come inside until the car gets here. You need to eat my friend. "His chair is in the back of the truck! Pary'on spoke up. The men got the chair out to put Guadalupe inside it. Cruz got on the phone making demands. Pary'on looked on as Cruz shot called. He knew Guadalupe really trusted and needed him. And he would be the loyal solider he needed. Thirty minutes late a Mayach Benz pulled up. Cruz escorted Guadalupe to the car himself. Cruz instructed Pary'on to get inside as well and give his remote to his G-Wagon to one of his men. He did not even argue, he just did what he was asked. Inside the car Cruz asked Guadalupe to finish telling him what was going on as they rode. Pary'on thought about how his last beef ended.......

CHAPTER 8

Mondo Ain't Going Out Like That

———— ❧ ————

Mondo heard about Pary'on power up around the city. Mondo had to move light because his name was around the city as a Green Light. And he moved around carefully. Mondo pulled up to this back page freaks house. She lived on Bayside project. A project that had history around the city for set up bitches. But he sat in his car getting skeed up. He hit the bag of cocaine hard. He watched all the movement around him. He clutched on his pistol looking around. He called the hoe on her phone. She answered on the second ring. "Come outside, I'm in the car, "he said throufh his teeth not being able to talk properly due to the amount of cocaine he was snorting. "Okay." He looke around at all the Christmas decorations all over. He could not evwn enjoy Christmas with his kids due to him beefing with Pary'on. But he had to do something. He watched as the prostitute came to the car. She jumpe in the passenger side with pajamas on. She had a big comforter cover wrapped around her body. Mondo pulled out his dick. Can I hit the bag? "She asked. He gave her a look like, bitch are you crazy! "I rather you pay me in white." "Alright." Mondo pulled out a big sandwich bag full of cocaine. He used a metal teaspoon to dip the bag of cocaine. Then she started looking around for something to put her coke in. "Do you got a bag or something?" "Naw." She seen his box of newport cigarettes then grabbed the box to pull off the plastic around the half empty box. She turned to the side to face Mondo holding open the plasic.

Mondo dumped more than enough coke inside the plastic. "Now come on." He told her as he grabbed his dick. She leaned over grabbing his dick to suck it. She began sucking his dick like a pro. As she sucked his dick he used his hand to slide inside the back of her pajama pants to rub her ass. He then let his fingers move to her wet pussy. "That's right suck that dick! OOhh yeah! You gonna let me fuck this pussy? He askes as his finger went deep inside her pussy, she answered. Em huh!" humming on his dick as she sucked. Mondo looked around as she sucked him odd. He notice the windows fogging up a little as their body heat mixed with heat coming from the car's vents. Mondo pulled his seat all the way back. "Hold up!" He lift up a little pulling his pants down. "Come on," he told her. She then began to strip out her pajamas pants. Once she was out her pants she climbed over to straddle him. Once she got comfortable she grabbed his dick then squat down on it. She began riding his dick like a true dick rider. A couple of niggas walked pass the car as they heard her moaning. They became nosey. They looked inside the car but kept the car kept moving. Mondo enjoyed the ride, but he kept his hand wrap around his pistol. As they kept fucking she started cumming, her pussy became stink smelling up the car wih a very thick unpleasant smell. Mondo held his breath to finish up with his nut. As he kept going on the smell became unbearing. He cracked the windows a little and it helped. He began taking control. He grabbed her hips holding her still while he hammered her pussy. He felt himself nutting, so he pushed himself up inside of her. After a few seconds he was drained. "Okay, get up and she crawled back over into the passenger side to begin putting her pajamas pants back on. Once she was situated she placed her bag of white inside her bra. "Can I have a cigarette? Mondo snatched the box from the dashboars frustrated. He pulle out two cigarettes. "Huh! Get the fuck out! Hurry up! "She got one foot out the car on the ground and Mondo began backing up.. "Damn nigga hold he fuck up!" "Hurry the fuck up bitch! And once she was out the car before she could close the door Mondo backed up fast the door closed slightly as he drove off. He slammed on brakes then reached over to close the door. He then got out of Bayside.

He was tired of ducking from these niggas. He had to go see his kids. He pulled up to his baby mother's house off Otranto Road. Even though it was three o'clock in the morning he still watched her house and parking lot before he pulled up. Pary'on done put an all-out man hunt on him. After he sat there sniffing coke for the next hour, he decided to go inside. Once inside he looked out the window clutching his pistol waiting for any sudden movement. After a while he went to his kid's room, and they were not in their room. So he went to his baby mother's room and saw his two kids in the bed with their mother in front of a portable fireplace that had the room warm. He did another look around sniffling as he walked around. He went into the bathroom in the hallway to wipe up before getting into the bed with his family. He finished, then walked around with his pistol again before he got inside the bed. His baby mama woke up looking violated until she seen that it was Mondo in her bed. "Baby! I love you! About time you came home! "She said in a sleepy voice. "Shhh! Lets just go to sleep! "He got comfortable, and his baby mama snuggled up against him. He melted in her ams. He felt himself drifting. His body was over tired. He had not slept in days. In minutes he was gone. The next morning Mondo jumped out of bed. He reached for his gun but it was gone. But, he was alone in the room. He jumped up. He looked at the alarm clock digits. It was 4:13 p.m. He slept for a long time. He hears the TV in the living room on, plus he heard his children's voice. When he walked in the living room his kids screamed. "DADDY!" Running up to him. His baby mother got up to hug him. "Where is my gun bae?" I put it up so the kids won't get it. "DADDY we about to put up our Christmas tree now, since your home! His youngest screamed. Let's do it." They put up the tree then the kids said, now we need some gifts to go under the tree. "Mondo spoke up quick. We gonna go shopping after I gwt something to eat. So go get yall shoes. "Yeah! They sccreamed running to go get their shoes. Mondo ate a healthy plate of leftovers from the night before of stew chicken and rice. They all got into his baby mother's Suzuki Farenza. They went to toys-r-us first. Mondo did not feel comfortable this close to shop because he could easily bump into someone he had beef with. So he decided to go shopping outside the area. They went to Mt. Pleasant to shop. As they visited all the stores they decided to go to Wal-Mart last since Wal-Mart never closes. So on their ride to Wal-Mart they looked at all the nice houses with lights. "Oooo Daddy we need to do our house like that. "Okay baby we are gonna get some lights from Wal-Mart to put on the house." "Yay!!! His baby mother loved Mondo presence with the kids, he was a dam good father. They got to Wal-Mart around 10:30 p.m. They shopped like it was a sweepstakes, filling up two buggies. Once they finally got all ringed up in the crowded store, their total came up to $2,643.00 dollars. They begin leaving the store with Mondo pushing one buggy and his baby mother pushing the other. The kids were gonna be squeezed up after all the bags got inside the car. As they were leaving the store the kids ran in front of their parents happy and skipping. Once they got check by the store employee at the exit and entrance they left out the store. As they finally got across the main strip to get to the parking lot the kids ran towards their mother's car leaving their parents. "Slow yall asses down! Come here now! Mondo screamed. The kids came running back towards their parents. A couple of Santa Claus walked around with charity buckets and fire fighter boots on to collect some money. One Santa with a big red children's bucket that was halfway full, stopped to ask Mondo and his baby mother for some money. "Care to donate to charity?" Mondo spoke for the family. "Of course, anything for the kids. "While Mondo stopped by the trunk of his baby mother's car she opened the trunk, and begin putting the bags inside. Mondo went inside his pocket to retrieve his knot of hundreds, fifties and twenties. Then the Santa pulled out a chrome nickel plated 44 mag and blew Mondo's brain all over his buggy of gifts. The baby mother screamed and the Santa zig zagged through the parking lot then jumped into a waiting all black Crown Vic. Leaving Mondo's family crying and screaming for help. JOB DONE!!

CHAPTER 9

More Beef 2 Cook

───────── ✧ ─────────

Pary'on thought back to the night he pulled the trigger ending his last beef. Now he was back at it again. He listened to Cruz and Guadalupe talk. Cruz was very powerful friend from what he understood of the conversation.. With them talking, Pary'on thought what he was gonna do to help Guadalupe out whatever he needed he would be there. They pulled up to a very nice mansion on a whole estate. The land was big. This how you suppose to live. As Cru's Maybach came to a halt in front of a tall black metal gate. Seconds later the gate begins to separate. The Maybach begins moving forward. As Pary'on looked from behind the curtains he notices all the workers begin waving as the Maybach slowly rolled past. The compound was the biggest Pary'on had seen. There were four houses on the compound. The main mansion had to be at least twelve thousands square feet. And Pary'on figured they were guest houses. As the Maybach made its way pass the two Olympic size pools, some were swimming and others were laying out on wooden lawn chairs sun tanning. Then they passed the tennis court were two beautiul women enjoyed a competiive match together. Then they came to a stop in front of one of the smalle houses. Then minurtes latee a nurse prsonnel came to the car rolling a wheel chair. This is your stop ol' friend, I'll be back to check up on you later. Their instructed to treat you better than they would treat me. Your strength has to be restored, so they will pump you full of steriods. I want to talk to Pary'on for a while. Then later we will come up with a plan to reverse these tables in this warfare we are up against. Do you want me to send for your wife and my god daughter?" GOD DAUGHTER! What the fuck! "Pary'on thought to himself. "Yes please do." It's done. Anything else? Not now my friend. I'm glad i have a friend like you in this troubled life." Cruz waved him off. "You would have done the same for me in a heart beat." "I sure would. Take care of my son Pary'on he is the son I never had." "I sure will. Not a hair on his head will be out of place in my presence my brother. Now go get some rest, my private jet will be sent to get your wife and daughter.By the time dinner is prepared your family will be here. Once again I'm sorry about Carlos. "Then the door opened for the nurse to do her job. Guadalupe was a very strong and he deserved a fair fight in this war. And he would defintely receive just that. Cruz's face straightened once he focused his attention on Pary'on. There goes a very dear friend of mine. He gave you his blessing so you must find out more about our enemy.

What can you inform me on what I don't know already? I got a text message from Isabella on the whole situation. As soon as I got to Guadalupe's he instructed me to bring him here. He sent for me so here I am now. "I have to speak to Isabella. She always been a tough cookie. "Tell me about it." Cruz smiled. Because she must have tested Pary'on's nuts. "She had some very good training. I need to speak to that ticking time bomb. "Cruz grabbed the car phone then dialed a number, seconds latr the other end answered. "I need a jet to go pick up Maria and Isabella now. They have to come here and don't take no for an answer. They both have to come by all means. He instructed Guadalupe's enforcers to be on call. Get with the floor general to make the proper arrangements. Then everyone report to the meeting hall. Keep me informed with any new changes. "Click..." Pary'on listened crefully to how Cruz made boss moves. He liked Cruz already. He sounded like him and Guadalupe been around each other forever. Because he sounded like Guadalupe. "What is your weapon of choice Pary'on?" I like Glock, nines and machine guns." "I will have you fully equip with your liking immediately." "Thank you." Cruz just nodded his head. The Maybach stopped in front of the main mansion. Then the door opened on both sides for Cruz and Pary'on to exit the car. Then Cruz directed his gaze towards the front gate. Pary'on followed his gaze to look down the long driveway to the front gate. He notices his G-Wagon in tow with three H2 Hummers. Then Cruz walked up to the front door of his mansion. The doors were both to greet him. "Hello Mr. Cruz." A maid sais "hola." I need you to add five extra for the table and let the chef know. "Will do Sensor

Cruz. "And the older looking Spanish maid walked off. "Follow me Pary'on and he walked behind Cruz. Pary'on notice Puerto Rican men armed wih assault rifles walking and green marble floors all through the mansion. The ceiling was out of reach, high with beautiful crystal chandeliers. The Study was the size of a master bedroom. Cruz looked out the fifteen foot glass window to gaze over his compound. Pary'on sat down in a very comfortable brown Italian leather chair with wood grain trim with shiny gold buttons. I'ma need you to gather up your suicide squad to assist us because if this was over drugs turf it will be a very bloody one. We are gonna need help. And people with their ears to the streets." "I got you on that. I have to visit a few good men I know." And I will provide you with men to go visit these soldiers your talking about, plus transporation you gonna have to move ike a real protected boss. I cannot risk losing you period. Lupe will really never forgive me. I heard your loyalty runs real deep for this life. So I will treat you just like Lupe's son. "They talked more and Cruz did not show it in his emotions, but he sees why Lupe called him his son. Pary'on outlook on things was just like that at his age. So he knew Pary'on was moving to great things in life. They talked for five hours They shared a lot of the same interests. "So you wanna play golf huh?" "I sure do. I see all the gentlemen with large amounts of money playing golf as a relaxing therapy session." Cruz laughed. "Well I have nine holes of rounds we can play and once we gain some type of control of this situation we are all in." "Fosho." i need to rally up the troops I got. Sometime within the next couple of days. They will take you anywhere you need to go." Then the desk phone rang. Cruz picked up on the second rin. "Holla." The person on the other end told Cruz, Isabella is loco, but we have both mother and daughter on flight to you." "Thank you. What did she do? She shot at all of us. She struck two of our men. She did not know who was trying ro enter her father's estate. But we have things under control. She wants to speak to you. "Let me speak to her." "Yes senor." Seconds past and Isabella was on the other end still raising hell speakinf Spanish a hundred miles per hour. Cruz smiled as he listened to Isabella talk sjot. "Hola." "Si Isabella." UNCLE CRUZ! "And Isabella started crying. "What's wrong my dear Isabella? But all she did was cry harder. So Cruz sat on the phone as she cried her sorrows away, "It's okay now! Help is here now! Thanks to Pary'on getting your father here safely! It's gonna be okay! We have to talk when you get here Isabella." "Si she responded. Cruz knew Guadalupe's wife Maria did not know what was really going on, but he had to speak to her to make sure she was okay for now. "Let me speak to your mother Isabella! Then Maria was on the phone. "Maria,

Como Estes?" "As good as I can be. How is my husband?" "He is okay. We all will talk when you get here." "Okay." Themano Senorettas." "Theamo Senor Cruz." Click..Cruz got up from his desk to fix himself a drink. Pary'on saw the hurt in Cruz's body lanuguage so he sat in silence as Cruz vented. They sat in complete silence for the next six hours playing chess on Cruz's immaculate chess board. They drank liquor and smoked weed in silence. Then there was a knock at the study's door. Cruz got up to open the door. Isabella and Maria was on the other side of that door. The ladies both hugged Cruz at the same time. Then tears flowed. After five minutes of embracing Isabella ran to Pary'on jumping into his embrace. She melted into his arms. Cruz could seen a different kind of affection between the two, They stood there for about ten minutes. "Let's go eat. Lupe will be joining us there." Cruz led the way to the big dining room.They sat there waiting for Guadalupe to arrive. Two body guards entered the room first before Guadalupe stumbled in wobbling with the cane he had in his right hand as he took each step. He felt a lot better. This was the first time he walked in weeks. Pary'on ran to his aid. He pulled out the chair at the other end of the table so Guadalupe could sit down. After Guadalupe sat down, Pary'on pushed his chair up towards the table. "Come Estes papa!" I'm mucho gwenos aqui. Gracias my hermanas!" Nadada my harmanos. "Cruz said. "Now that we are all here, who is our opposing threat? Guadalupe took over. "It's the diablo cartel." Cruz had a feeling. "EL Tarpeta has struck my main enforcer my paketa harmanos Carlos. Then they tried to get Isabella. My car was booby trapped as well. "Isabella was about to have the shock of her life. EL Tarpeta is mad that I am Isabella's father." "What!" Isabella screamed. Pary'on heard the story before by Carlos. He just kept it to himself. "Yeah Isabella I took your mother from him thirty-seven years ago. Your mothcr became pregnant with you after two years of me and her creeping around on him. Me and EL Tarpeta were friends once he let the money he was receiving from America go to his head, We all were in Mexico until he made it to Texas as me and your mother got caught by border patrol. We fought one of the officers that tried to put cuffs on your mother. After I hit the border patrol officer we ran then jumped in the river to swim back to Mexico. Me and your mother waited months to hear from EL Tarpeta. He got in contact with his parents then his parents got in contact with your mother, who was three months pregnant with you. EL Tarpeta parents told him he would e a daddy. So he begin sending money back to your mother, and his parents. Me and your mother became lovers as time went by. She just did not know who your father was. So when you were born it was plain as daylight that he was not your father. So his parents begin making threats to your mother and I was not going for it. So your Uncle Carlos shot EL Tarpeta's father and we all came to the states. We all started hanging with the local Mexicans in Texas making money. But we did not begin making real moves until we took over The Paso Cartel and our family became in power. And we ended up taking over a couple of empires to strengthen up our cartels so we could not be touched so easily. Now, EL Tarpeta struck when the time was right. He has two other cartels that have been plotting revenge on the Paso cartel forever." We are not going out like that! I have a large group of solid friends that belong to the Bloods! And for that work, i can get all the help we need! I'm heading out for Atlanta in the morning. I will have a large group of killers ready for war as soon as I get word to my people. "Cruz interrupted Pary'on. "We need Bloods with jurisdiction in Texas and New Mexico." "Man fuck jurisdiction! They kill my brother and tried to take out my family! All of this over jealousy! A fucking hater! Well, I'm going head first about mine! I need to know these muthafuckas whereabouts! So we can start eliminating these sorry bitches until we can cut the head off! If I catch EL Tarpeta before yall, I will torture him and his kids! Lets get to work!

I want blood spill over Texas and New Mexico! And blood will be flowed! We have to be smart! But our presence will be felt! I need as much information i can get on his Diablo Cartel! Because I need to put my people on point! Let's start planning after dinner! It's a war on us! And I'll be damn if I don't participate in all the fun! If it is smoke they want, its smoke they'll get!" Cruz like Pary'on as the minutes ticked. There was nothing else to be said. So they enjoyed a nice dinner in silence.. The maid cleared the table then brought on the desert. Maria fed her husband the very rich cheese cake with strawberries soaked in strawberry syrup. She rubbed her husband's back whispering into his ear kissing him. Isabella loved looking at her parents. They were so much in love. Isabella laid her head on Pary'on's shoulder relaxing, rubbing her stuffed stomach. Pary'on was very upset at the fact Carlos was not there anymore. "Get up sweetie," Pary'on mumbled to Isabella. He then got up and excused himself. He walked to the exit where the guards were standing outside the door. They gave him a look that asked him where was he going. Pary'on looked them up and down with ice cold stare then kept moving past the heavy armed men. They looked at their boss Cruz to receive any kind of sign to fuck Pary'on up. But Cruz waved them off. Cruz looked at Guadalupe and Guadalupe picked up on the look. He kissed his wife then got up. "Come on Cruz." And the men walked through the house to find Pary'on. Pary'on walked outside on the top balcony. He did not even look back when he heard foot steps behind him. Tears just trickled down his cheeks as he thought about Carlos. Carlos was the reason he was living the life he was living. He wanted revenge bad. Isabella wrapped her arms around Pary'on waist. She rested the side of her face on his back. She began crying as well. This was the first time she could remember feeling her family powerless. The feelin was very terrifying. They were outnumbered for sure. Minutes later Cruz and Guadalupe walked up. "Bella let us speak with Pary'on, Guadalupe said. She turned around with tears in her eyes. Her father hugged her. "It's gonna be alright my Bella! Trust me! "He said rubbing her back." "I hope so father! "I hope so!" She said sadly. "Go help your mother out Bells. We have to get down to business and she left moping. After Isabella was gone, the men sat down in the chairs. Pary'on I feel that you are very passionate about Carlos, but we can't move reckless either. See if you can find him before us. EL Tarpeta is at this height right now. We can get close to the Diablo Cartel but my people in Texas cannot move until we are gonna capitalize on seizing the moment to bring EL Tarpeta down. Diablo Cartel have a sign that they have to let you know its them. Its the Mexican flaf with horns of the devil on it or a devil head with a Mexican flag around it or the letters D.C....The head honchos are easy to find, but hard to kill. There ruthless killers. They are Bato Locos forever. We have to have a private affair for Carlos because we got infiltrated. So Carlos body will be buried next to our parents. Only the house soidiers can be trusted. Anyone that was in the field we can't use. We have not found out the leak yet but we have enough trained shooters to make some type of noise. Now that Cruz is with us we should be ready for any type of war. "I'm heading out in the morning to meet up with my people; where in New York do I bring my team? Cruz spoke up. "If they are friends o yours they are friends of ours. So bring your top ten soliders here and I'll have my people merge with the others you bring." I have Muslims and Bloods. So once I'm in the big apple, who do I contact?" "My chief of security.He will be there before you pull out in the morning. The car you take will have a speed dial of 1,2 and 3. #1 is me, #2 is my chief security and #3 is my compound security. So you will be good. And once we get everyone together we will then strategize our attack move." They talked for two more hours before they retreated to their bedrooms. The next morning Pary'on woke up with a purpose. He went outside to find Jorge waiting along with five serious looking men that was muscle bound. "My name is Jorge and I'm speed dial #2. These five men will be accompanying you on your ride. The driver will go where ever you say go. These men will treat you like they would treat Mr. Cruz. Have a nice trip down South." "I plan on it." And Pary'on got inside the stretch Phantom limo. They made it to Atlanta, Georgia in twelve hours. They pulled up in front of this mini mansion in Buckhead. The driver stopped in front of the entrance to the driveway. He called the phone in the back where Pary'on was and Pary'on picked up. "Yea." Mr. Pary'on do you want me to pull up in the driveway?" "Yea." The driver did as he was told. They stopped next to a fleet of red cars. Pary'on jumped out decked down in Louis Vuitton from head to toe. With some Louis Vuitton shades. He walked up to the door then rang the doorbell. Minutes later Chill answered the door. "What the fuck!" "Yea, man it's me! And they dapped then embraced. "Come in my nigga. "Pary'on looked at the car and waved the men to come inside. Chill looked at the heavy armed men that looked like mecenaries walk towards them. Either you're the president of another country or some shit is about to be reveales to me." "The second guess sounds about right Pary'on told Chill. Chill was 6'2 and brown skin weighing about 225. He was all chill mode until he got mad. Then you would be telling him to chill out. "Well come tell me homie!" They went inside Chill's nice living quarters. Chill looked at the men standing behind Pary'on. He knew Pary'on was on another level, but this nigga had really stepped his game up. He had real bodyguards. "I did some research about some shit goin on in the streets of Texas and New Mexico with your Bloods. I know you are up in ranks throughout the United States with this Bloody life." "So what do you need me to do my friend? It's been a very long time since we both played in the streets." "I need you to make some calls to Texas and New Mexico about the Diablo Cartel. I need whereabouts, who's in charge from the top to the bottom. They killed Carlos in retaliation due to Guadalupe takinf a woman from a Cartel Don thirty-seven years ago. And they struck the Paso Cartel killing Carlos and trying to kill Isabella and her mother. So this Don name EL Tarpeta. "Chill eyes got big at EL Tarpeta's name. "Do you know him homie?" I had some run ins with them a few years ago, They rolled through the streets of Atlanta, South Carolina and Savannah. I know Lil Donald and Lil Man ran the group of Diablo Cartel Mexicans from the streets of Charleston. They came around there setting up shop, and you know how that is around the way. They even kill eight of them Mexicans. Lil Donald got shot. They kill Lil Man's brother Snoop on a kickdoor. I remember them niggas got away with a lot of work and money. Snoop killed three of them Mexicans in a big standoff so Lil Man ans Lil Donald could get away. He could have gotten away to, but he lost control of his motorcycle and went head first with a garbage truck. He got up staggering trying to get away but the Mexicans gunned him down. "Pary'on shook his head." "I heard about that. But I did not know it was Diablo Cartel. Everyone talked good about Snoop going out like that. And I remember they ran all the Mexicans out from around the way after that. I need to get in contact with them too. I'm sure they want some action. Well I got two of my top ten with them. They always look for smoke. Do you got their numbers?" I can get them over here in a few hours." Do that for me. "Plus let me make some calls to New Mexico and Texas." "Alright." Just like that Chill and Lil Man and Lil Donald was on their way. But he had to put in a little work to get his Bloods on the job. He called Thugga too. Less than hour Chill was talking to the Big Homie over New Mexico and he agreed to meet up with Chill and Pary'on as soon as they could get to New York.

Now iit was time for business. Pary'on like affirmative action. Now he had one more person to talk too. He pulled out his personal cell phone to search through his contacts. He found Hakim number. He pressed the little phone in the corner. Hakim answered the phone on the fourh ring. "Asalamiakim!" "Malakinsalon." What's up Akie?" "I need some physical help Akie. I know I can count on you. Your assistance is needed Akie. "Inshalloah Akie. Alhamdulillah." I need a army of men Akie to help my family. The Diablo Cartel have been a thorn in my side and enough is enough." "Allah Akbah Akie. I will meet you soon, I'ma give you an address to meet up. Bring at least twenty of your best men." "Will do, send me the information ASAP! "As soon as we end this call." "I love you my brother. End it now. "And Pary'on ended the call sending Hakim the address to Guadalupe's compound. He had everyone to go to Guadalupe's compound. He was gonna strike back. The next day everyone was at Guadalupe's compound ready. Chill has so much of his Bloods on deck ready. It was at least thirty Bloods, twenty-five Muslims and all the enforcers Jorge had along with the guards from the Paso compound. Pary'on had to strike back for Carlos. Pary'on parked the Phantom in the middle of all his men. He stood on top of the Phantom's hood. "We are gonna strike every spot Diablo has. They have a few clubs here in Texas and two in New Mexico. They have a bike club here in Texas outside of San Antonio. We are gonna kill everyone. If we can get a few of them to talk, get them to talk. We need to find out as much as possible on EL Tarpeta. Half of us willl hit Texas and the other half will hit New Mexico. Make the shit count. Hit them hard. EL Tarpeta's right hand man in New Mexico house is under surveillance right now. Me, Chill, Thugga, Lil Donald and little Man along with Jorge will hit his spot. We all meet up back here in two days. Be safe men. Make this shit count. Let's GO! And everyone moved. Chill, Thugga, Lil Donald and Lil Man stood by Jorge. Everyone had a sergeant from the field to direct the men at war in the field. "Let's go hit Enrique spot hard. He will tell us something. Jorge said. They all got into the H 3 Hummer. Jorge had bullet proof vest to go roll on Enqurie. "Did you bring my outfit Jorge?' Jorge pulled out a pair of all black air force ones and all black attire. As they rode to Enquire's mini mansion, Pary'on changed into his war clothes. They drove eight hours to the outside of Enquire's mini mansion. It was pitch black dark when they exited the H 3 Hummer. Their eyes got use to the night. It was a dry and ho night. It was so quiet you could hear the coyotes howling at the full moon. Shadow figures could be seen walking the perimeter of the mansion's yard. Jorge lead the way with his night vision googles. He moved swiftly running up on the first man. He hit him with a seven piece martial art move that killed the man instantly. He disarmed the dead body. He gave the rifle to Chill. Chill put the extra rifle on his shoulders as he held his machine gun. They ran across the yard then squat down once they were against the house. Jorge whispered to Lil Man, "one of the men is coming your way. Stab him in the back of his neck. Once he walked pass, he passed the Rambo knife. Lil Man's heart was beating out his chest. He begin sweating under his arms, his adrenaline was racing. They all heard the man approaching. As he walked pass, Lil Man ran up on the man with his arm raised with rhe knife in his hand. He bought the knife down on the back of the man's neck. The knife sliced through his skin like a butter knife through butter. Lil Man let the knife stay in the man as his body dropped to the ground. He began rolling around in the grass dying. He tried to scream but he could not due to the blood flowing out his mouth.

Pary'on ran to the body then dragged the dead body over towards them. He snatched the knife out and then blood sprayed a little then began pouring out. He disarmed the man as well. "Let's move! Jorge said a little above a whisper. He moved to the side door. He tried it and it was locked. Then a light came on brightening up the area they were in. They ran around the house to get away from the light before he was seen. Then a few voices could have been heard speaking Spanish, Jorge understood what they said. "Let's move! Their coming! "And they ran up the side steps to the second layer of the mini mansion. "Let's go in! Fuck it! Just stay together! Pary'on said shooting the glass wooden door to enter the house. They busted the door down easily entering the spot. They all had their guns drawn aiming in front of them. Some men ran towards them so they all open fire killing the four men. "Go towards them! I believe Enrique is over there or close!" They stopped in front of a big double door. Thugga kicked the door open; Enrique was in his night clothes along with his wife. Enrique had a pistol in his hand once he seen the men he shot two times missing his target. ENRIQUE STOP! for we kill you and your family! "Pary'on shouted. He shot Enrique in the leg dropping him. His wife screamed. Chill pistol whipped his wife knocking her out. "Lil Dondald and Lil Man, yall tie them up. We will be back. Don't move until we get back. "Jorge told them. "Come on we have to get the kids. "And the rest of them ran to the other rooms. They got the two daughters of Enrique and his wife. "Let's get back to he Hummer. "Jorge instructed. Pary'on grabbed Enrique. Chill grabbed the wife, Thugga had one of the daughters and Jorge had the other. "Lil Donald you and Lil Man have to shoot our way out here back to the H 3. Let's go! "Pary'on told them, Lil Donald and Lil Man to lead the way with their assault rifles aimed forward as they lead the group in the hallway. Everyone had their victims on their shoulders running like in the army. The heavy of the four was Enrique's wife. "Look at the men coming up the stairs! "Chill shouted to Lil Donald and Lil Man and they let their AR-15 loose making the men that was not hit run for cover. Then Pary'on, Jorge, Thugga and Chill ran out the door they came in. When they hit the steps they dropped two of them. Enrique rolled down to the bottom of the steps screaming in pain. His wife stopped halfway down the steps. Chill picked her back up. "Let's move! Jorge said running towards the yard side entrance they came in. Gunfire rained around the yard. They did not stop. Lil Donald returned fire letting the AR-15 shoot in the direction of the gun shots. Pary'on grazed in the shoulder causing him to drop Enrique. He eventually fell with him. But he crawled to safety dragging Enrique with him. They made it outside the yard to the street. They were almost to the Hummer, Pary'on got up to his feet then picked a screaming fightin Enrique up. He ended up punching Enrique in his face a few times knocking him out. He picked him up pulling him to the H 3 Hummer. "Get your bitch ass in there." He yelled at Enrique as he picked him up slamming him inside the back of the Hummer. Once he slammed the back door then jumped inside. Jorge was in the driver's seat. He put the Hummer in reverse then punch the gas. The Hummer swerved backwards away from Enrique's mini mansion. Jorfe hit a smaller car as he drove forward turning around to leave out. He notice men running down the streets trying to gun down the Hummer. He finally gained control of the Hummer then he smashed the gas leaving the men behind chasing the Hummer. As they rode in silence no one said a word until the sign on the side of 1-10 east read: Texas 15 miles." Change cars Jorge. We are gonna blindfold everyone then we are going to Cruz's estate where Guadalupe is. We will get as much as we can out of everyone. Don't call no one. I'll get with Cruz first and foremost to see where we will take Enrique.

So after we switch cars, we will go to Cruz's estate. We are going to get something out of his family. "Pary'on crawled to the front. He grabbed the car phone he hit the number #1 then send. Cruz picked up on the second ring. "Talk to me." Cruz voice sounded concern. "This is Pary'on, I have some good news to report. "Okay" Cruz answered eagerly to know. "We have Enrique and his family in the car with us right now. He was shot in the leg so we need him alive to torture his ass. I also was shot in the shoulder. But i does not hurt that bad. It burns like a cut. We are gonna blindfold everyone then bring them to your estate. "Cruz smiled. "We were worried sick about you. You should at least tell us the moves you were making. Never the less you handled it well. i will inform Lupe. Isabella can't be found. She ran off yesterday. But report to us ASAP! "Will do." Click...Pary'on grabbed his cell phone to call Isabella. He called her phone three times with no answer, so he texted her:

Isabella, I know shit has been krazy, but you can't be disappearing like that. HMU ASAP. I hope your safe, Sent 2:16 p.m.

Pary'on waited and nothing. Not even a reply. So he did what he said he was gonna do. They got to Guadalupe's compound at 6:25 a.m. They pulled everyone out the hummer. They were laid out on the concrete tied up. Pary'on went inside to get everyone something to drink. He got some scarfs to blindfold Enrique and his wife and kids. Once they were blindfolded he had them in the Phantom ready to go see Guadalupe. One of Jorge's bodyguards stood watch while everyone ate and freshen up. When Pary'on went to look at the hummer, now that it was daylight out he had the inside cleaned by one of the house workers. The worker brought Pary'on his phone along with guns. He notices his notifications sign blinking. He checked it, and it was a message and a miss call from Isabella. The message read:

I am okay. Thank you for showin me you care. I was beginning to think I had to kidnap someone else you loved to get your attention. Where do you wanna meet me at? Received at 5:53 a.m.

Pary'on called her phone and she answered. "Your still fucking krazy! Where are you? "I am at the Ritz Carlton in New York. "Go back to your mother and father. I'll be leaving out from yall estate in Texas in a few. I'm going to Cruz compound. I have Enrique EL Tarpeta and right hand man." He is the one that tried to kill me! I can't wait to see him. So help me GOD! "Well we are gonna get some information from him before we kill him okay. "She loved how Pary'on just ran shit. "I'll see you back there, go back now! And he hung up without letting her saying a word. He thought back when Isabella kinapped his little freak business partner Gina. After Isabella let her go, she vowed to never fuck with Pary'on again. He had to much girl problems. She almost lost her life fucking with Isabella. And Isabella cut her long pretty hair. The money or Pary'on's dick was not worth her life. She wanted to contact him bad, but Isabella threats were loud and clear, plus the dick was the best she had but her life is what she valued more. So she never spoke to Pary'on again. Pary'on gathered all types of reports about their strike back. A lot of houses got hit, robbed a lot of people got killed during this Paso Cartel's raid, now tha is how you bomb back. EL Tarperta had to come out of hiding soon. His right hand man was now held for ransom just so he could out of hiding and top enforcer got killed at their bike club. Sooner or later he would send a messge to Guadalupe bes rasscause he got hit hard. This raid hurt, it was not about the money. But they retrieved four hundred nmillion dollars. Jorge's sergeant that went on the hit with Bloods and Muslims caught the shipment of US currency to Mexico. There was no way EL Tarpeta did not feel this in his accounts. The money was brought to Cruz by the sergeant. When Pary'on and Jorge made it to New York along with Chill, Thugga, Lil Donald and Lil Man, Cruz and Guadalupe was waitin along with Isabella. When the Phantom stopped in front of Cruz, he was smilinf from ear to ear. When Pary'on got out of the car with a half nake Enrique in tow, then his family was escorted behind him towards Cruz, Guadalupe and Isabella. "Pary'on my boy!" You are amazing! I heard how you came up with this last minute plan! And you had real success coming through! "Guadalupe and Cruz was dressed up in army fatigues and boots, Guadalupe was impressed at Pary'on. Cruz had a Gucci suitcase sitting next to him. He picked it up then handed it to Pary'on. "This three hundred million dollars out of the four hundred. Split this with your friends. Let them know I said, "Thank you. I'm sure we can handle the rest. I'm sure this should be enough for them. Plus me and Guadalupe will provide some drugs as well. We thank everyone, but I think we can handle the rest of this war. Go bless your people Pary'on, then come back here we have some unfinish business with rhis piece of shit! We will keep you posted until you come back." "Okay." I know they will appreciate all of this. Pary'on then went to Jorge to shake his hand." I needed you out there and you were an awesome partner. Five million of this money belongs to you too. Come with me to separate it all then distribute it all to my fam." Jorge looked at Cruz for validation and he nodded his head. Pary'on, Chill, Lil Donald and Lil Man along with Jorge got back into the Phantom and the driver pulled off. Cruz looked at Guadalupe. "Now there goes a very loyal black man. He is the best of his kind. He has heart, loyalty, love and brains." That's my son I never had. He will go far and grow old in this lifestyle. Now lets handle this piece of shit. They pushed them to the backyard. They went into a small house looking shed. Once inside, their blindfolds were taken off. Guadalupe smiled at the shocking look on Enrique's face. Enrique looked over at his wife and two daughters. Then he looked up at Guadalupe who was looking at all the wonderful things he could use to torture answers out of them. Cruz and his guards tied Enrique upside down by his ankles. Please don't do this Guadalupe! Do you hear me! But Guadalupe just ignored Enrique's wife. Guadalupe turned around with a hammer and Louisville slugger brand new wooden bat. Can you please just tell him what he wants Enrique?! Cruz tied the oldest daughter to a chair. Then his wife stood up. Guadalupe swung the bat as hard as he could connecting with her knee cap. Her whole leg turned to jell-o. She screamed loud in agony. Her kids begin crying. Then they went to the oldest child that was tied to the chair then grabbed her right hand then made her spread her hand out on the table. Guadalupe smashed her palm with the ball of the hammer. Her hand cracked out loud as her bones were crushed. Her hand brust open with blood. She passed out from the pain. Her parents thought she was dead the way she fainted from the pain. Enrique begin yelling. "OK! OK! What do you want to know?! Please leave them alone! Please!"

Cruz snatched the bat from off the floor. He rushed to Enrique. He barley hit Enrique in his nuts with the handle part of the bat and Enrique screamed in pain. "Now what do you have to say?! Enrique cried in pain. "What do you know?! "He kicked Enrique in the stomach. Being upside down was getting to him. He felt the blood oozing down his nose. He couldn't swallow at all. So as he tried to talk it was a bunch of gibberish. So they tilt him up enough for him to spit out his mouth full of blood. He then begin to cough out spraying blood all over. "Talk you bitch! Now! "Wha-Wh -What do you wanna know!? WHERE IS EL TARPETA?" He begin crying out trying to plea, but Guadalupe punched him in his face before he could lie. "Stop lying! Where is he? "Then Guadalupe grabbed a box of salt, he began pouring salt inside Enrique's daughter's hand. "She screamed out loud. "AHHGHH! PAPA TELL HIM! Please PAPA!" Then Enrique screamed, "In Keywest! Keywest, Flordia! Guadalupe looked at Cruz smiled shrugging his shoulders. "Directions." The Castle. It's the biggest house there on the island. "For your sake you better not be lying! Cruz looked at Guadalupe. We are gonna keep yall here until we go get EL Tarpeta. I told you the truth man! At least give us time to run from Diablo! They'll kill my family! I told you where he was! Guadalupe untied the rope to drop Enrique. Enrique fell hard to the floor. Guadalupe kicked him repeatedly. He choppe him in his foot with the hammer. Enrique bones cracked. His screams echoed out loud. "Watch them all. "Cruz instructed to his security. Guadalupe and Cruz left out the room. They got ready to go to Key West, Flordia

CHAPTER 10

Split the Pot

Pary'on and Jorge finally split up the three hundred million dollars. Now they went around giving everyone five million dollars a piece. This was the biggest pay off for them, for free. A couple Bloods and Muslims died during the battle. So Pary'on made sure their families got their share of the money. They finish delivering all the money when an eerie feeling came across Pary'on causing him to shiver. Jorge saw Pary'on and asked him, are you ok my friend!" Then Pary'on saw a Mexican following them. Pary'on made four left turns in a row, which was a complete circle. "Don't panic but there is a Mexican followinf us. I'm about to lead him to a trap. "Pary'on grabbed his phone calling Skeet. Skeet answered fast. "Yo what's up big bruh?" I'm coming to Wild Game Road and there are some Mexicans in a black Scion box truck following me. I'ma give yall time to get ready to Swiss cheese them. After we pass you, begin to Swiss cheese it up." "Gotcha." Pary'on drove towars Wild Game Road taking the long way. When they got on Wild Game Road, Pary'on seen a car parked on the side of the road in the grass with its hazzard lights on. He sped up a little to give himself a little distance apart. He was about to pass Skeet and Rudy when he watched them get their guns ready. Skeet had two pistols and Rudy had a pistol grip pump. He mashed rhe gas then the gunfire sounded off the quiet country road. The Mexicans lost control and flipped the Scion. As the Scion flipped two times it got stopped bya tree. Pary'on slammed on brakes throwing the car in reverse. He grabbed the back of the passenger's head rest then looked backwards smashing the gas as he drove back toards the crash Scion with Skeet and Rudy and a Mexican jumped out with a Mac 11 shooting at Skeet, Rudy and the car. As he was shooting, he was always running backwards. One of he bullets struck Skeet in the face dropping him backwards in the middle of the road. Pary'on slammed on brakes parking the car hopping out with his nine millimeter Beretta in hand letting the clip ride as he ducked down in front of the car for protection. But the Mexicans got away running into the nearby woods. Jorge got out then ran up to the Scion Box car as Pary'on and Rudy tend to Skeet. Skeet's body was shaking as if he was having a seizure. Blood was everywhere. "He is dead Rudy! Let's go! Get into the car and go!' Jorge saw two Mexicans inside the upside Scion that was bleeding from their heads and faces. He still emptied his clip into both Mexicans. He ran back to the truck waiting on Pary'on. Pary'on looked down at Skeet that was no longer shaking. His nerves jerked his body every now and then. Pary'on could not control it; he shedded tears for his best friend. he took Skeet's chain and his favorite ring and bracelet off his dead body. He looked at the brain matter that was under Skeets leaking head. he secured the jewerly then ran to the car where Jorge was waiting. "Hurry up Pary'on! Undalay, Undalay!" Pary'on jumped inside the driver's side seat then put the car in drive. His right foot smashed down the accelerator, and the car up to enormous speed, Pary'on could not stop the tears from running down his face. He felt gulity for Skeets death. He made his way to Mrs. Pinkney house in the Green Hurst neighborhood. Pary'on slowed down a few houses from Skeet's mother's house. He hope she would not have been home right now, but her burgundy 2018 Town and Country Chrysler Van was right in the driveway. When Pary'on pulled into the driveway, Mrs. Pinkney was inside her flower bed planting multiple flowers. She smiled once she looked up from planting a small plant when her eyes looked on Pary'on behind the front windshield of the car that parked in her driveway ten feet away from her. Jorge sat still in the passenger seat as he watched Pary'on approached the lady dressed in leisure clothes with an oversized straw hat on her head. She had on some thick oversized gloves that looked as if they were put to ten years of use. She still hugged Pary'on carefully not letting her gloves touch his clothes. She then notices Pary;on start to explain that her son was just murdered. Pary'on had to catch Mrs. Pinkney's limp body before it hit the concrete of the walkway. Pary'on shook his head as he picked up Mrs. Pinkney to take her to a safe spot. He places her in a big lawn chair until she came too.

Once she finally gains her consciousness, she began crying. Through her sobs she tried to get out a surprise she had for them all. "Damon...! She began having the hic-ups trying to talk. "Damon....! Go inside! "She pointed to the house. Pary'on ran inside the house he has been in millions of times since he was friends with Skeet and D-Block. And as he step foot inside the house he heard some music coming from the living room. When he ran inside he living room he seen D-Block turned around fast flinching a bit, His mouth full of gold teeth, smiled at the sight of his longtime friend Pary'on. They hugged each other tightly. They rocked back-n-fourth holding each other. "Damn boy it's been a long time! I have to spoil his moment through! Skeet just got gun down! What!" Then Pary'on explained what happen. "So where do we go from here bruh? Come with me. I hate to leave Mrs. Pinkney like this." "Let's go get her. "Mrs. Pinkney had come inside as Pary'on explained what happen. She went to her room. They went to close the door and they put their ears to the room door and they could hear Mrs. Pinkney praying. So they waited for her to finish. She was a mother figure to them all. They knocked on the door then entered. Mrs. Pinkney walked up to them both with her Bible anointed oil in hand. "Sit." She said pointing to her huge king size canopy bed. They both sat down next to each other. She begins her ritual. She got her prayer water then poured some inside her hand then flicked her fingers showering both of their faces. Then she got her oil to put a dab on her two fingers then drew a cross on their foreheads. She began speaking in tongue. She started reading out the bible speaking Hebrew language. This went on for the next ten minutes. "Be bless my children. God has his shield around you both. Let the Lord fight this war. I don't need any more pain from these wicked streets. I love you boys! Please! NO More of this! Let the Lord and Savior fight this battle. "They could not even lie to her. They had to seek revenge for Skeet. It's only right. Because he would do the same for them. So D-Block and Pary'on just put their heads down as they walked out of the house. They got inside the car to make their way to Cruz house. When they made it to Cruz compound D-Block was at a loss for words. When they pulled up to the gate, he read about this type of life in books and seen it on movies, but actually living this was gonna be amazing. I'm so glad you're my friend Pary'on! Damn! What the fuck! Yall niggas turned up for real bruh!" Pary'on shook his head smiling. They all got out then went inside. Pary'on explained to Cruz who D-Block was. Cruz smiled with his platinum smile. "Welcome to my house." "House! This is a CASTLE FIT FOR A KING! D-Block said shaking Cruz's hand. "Naw this bullshit shack. "Cruz smiled after he made his sarcastic comment. "Well make yourself at home my friend. Pary'on, Guadalupe would like to see you once you get your friend settle inside. "Ok!" Tell him I will be there within an hour." "Will do." And they went their separate ways. "They treat you like you're their boss bruh. "D-Block said as they walked inside. "We brothers man. That's all I see. They act as if you're on their level. "Pary'on looked at Block, because I am. Then they walked ahead of him to show him to the room he would be sleeping in. "We will go shopping tomorrow. So don't worry about clothes. We will give Skeet the best funeral ever. I just had to get you from all that for now. We will mourn my dawgs death. Everyday he'll be missed. Get settled, I'll be back. I have to go. "Alright!" They dapped up then Pary'on went to his room. He could of hear his phone going off then it stop ringing before he could get to it. He raced to his personal cell phone that was on top of the dresser still attached to his charger. It was his wifey Marie. She called him sixty-eight times, includin twenty-two text messages. He called back ASAP. He missed his wifey. This was the first time she reached out to him since she walked out with the kids. Marie picked up on the first ring. Pary'on was shocked by her screaming in the phone. "They got Tania! "Who?" "Come home baby! Please! She is gone and they want to speak to you in order to get her back!" I'm coming now!" Pary'on ran to Guadalupe, I have to go! They have my lil sister! It only can be EL Tarpeta! I have to go! Pary'on ran to Cruz. "I need your private jet to take me to Miami Now!" Then he explained what happen to Cruz." "I'll have the driver take you to the landing strip. Call me ASAP to inform us what is going on. "I will." Cruz watched Pary'on get into the car to go to his family. Cruz then pulled out his phone to speed dial someone. "Follow Pary'on to Miami. Protect him with all cost. "Click...Two hours later Pary'on pulled up to the airport. Marie met him there. She had the kids with her waiting on the landing strip. Once the kids seen their daddy, they screamed out. "DADDY!" And came running to him. Marie was right behind them. They all gave him a group hug once he walked down the steps to the private jet. Marie began crying. He hugged them tight. He missed his family. They walked to the car to go home. Once Pary'on goes inside the car he took out the wand Cruz gave him to check for planted bugs or GPS transmitters. None was in the car. He went inside the glove box to retrieve a loaded 9 mm Rutgers. Marie gave him the card. He opened it and it was a small paragraph typed message and it said:

Pary'on,

This is EL Tarpeta. We need to meet on respectfully terms. Don't contact anyone or Tania is Dead! Just me and you! We have to negoiate Real Business! Come to the club CREAMY. At the front door tell them you're Pary'on, and they'll escort you to me. Come by Saturday or the deal is OFF!

Pary'on close the card. He breathed out heavy. Marie just sniffled and had the hiccups as she cried. It's gonna be alright baby. Tania will be back. Calm down. Daddy is home. "Pary'on kept looking in the sun visor mirror at three cars that has now been behind them for the last four blocks. Pary'on never took his eyes off the mirror as he told Marie, "Take four lefts baby." Marie knew what that meant. She looked in the rearview mirror at the cars behind them. "Oh baby! What is going on? Why is this happening? What did you do? Or who did you piss off? Pary'on remained calm. "Just drive baby everything will be okay. "He said as he checked the pistol clip. The first three turns the driver was behind them still. Then he knew it. "Pull over! Before the car could of stop all the way, Pary'on was out the car pointing his gun at the cars that was now turning the corner. The first car slammed on brakes at the sight of Pary'on's pointing his gun. Then all the doors open up. Then Jorge and the rest of the security jumped out the car. "We were told to keep an close eye on you. And it isn't no option. "Boy, YALL CAN'T DO THAT SHIT! I was ABOUT TO OPEN FIRE! "We are here for you and your family. "Well follow us. Pary'on got back inside the car. They with me." Then they made it to his mini mansion, the men surrounded the premises. Marie looked around at the action of the men that followed Pary'ons commands. She knew that her husband was now in a different tax bracket. They went inside to Marie's whole immediate family was inside. The energy was so dull. But when Pary'on, Marie and the kids walked inside their spirits picked up of the sight of Pary'on. Jorge told ten soliders the orders in Spanish. "Check the house for bugs and protect everyone in here with your life! Jorge looked at Pary'on! We will check the house for bugs and we will protect everyone as long as you ask us to. The outside of the house will be on guard twenty-four seven. "Thats what's up. Then he passed the card to Jorge. Jorge read it then passed it back. "i'm going tonight. A coupe of people need to go there a few hours before me. I have to bring her back home. The family began crying out loud as they heard Pary'on even mentioned Tania. "Roger that." Later that night....Pary'on dressed for the occasion. He gave his challenger car keys to the valet personnel. He like the vies the club gave the Atlantic Ocean. The vale driver gave Pary'on a car ticket chip. Pary'on walked up to the door. A gorgeous Spanish looking woman asked him, VIP or regular. I'm Pary'on. Her eyes got big. "Hold on!" Minutes later six men came walking up to Pary'on. Follow us. Three led the way and three was behind him so close if he stopped walking thy would bump into him. They escorted him to a backdoor. Then they walked into a back allyway where a stretch Mercedes Benz Van was pulling up. It stopped in front of the men. The side door opened and the front three men made way for Pary'on to jump inside the luxury plush Van. Inside were EL Tarpeta and three women. One of them being Tanis. At the sight of Pary'on she began crying. Have a seat Pary'on!" "EL Tarpeta pointed to the empty comfortable seats. EL Tarpeta was not tall at all. But he had his hair slick back in a ponytail. He had a very expensive tailor made suit on along with some gator loafers. His all gold Rolex was flooded with diamonss. He ws sipping some bourbon. The women were dressed very elegant. But he knew it was more to them than their beauty. The van begins moving. "See I am very fair man. Pary'on. I have done a very thorough investigation on you. Your very loyal and trustworthy. Now your friend Cruz and Guadalupe, I can not speak to fond of them. You're more powerful than meets the eye. I don't trust Cruz or Guadalupe, but you are a different type of man. I'm very sorry what happen to your friend Skeet. He was becoming a very loyal businessman for me. "The look on Pary'ons face said it all.

"Oh you did not know. Did notice how Skeet was not reing up anymore with you huh? It's because he got into the heroin business with me. He talked about how jealous he was of you. "Pary'on head began spinning thoughts. That's how we found your family in Miami. He just would not trade in your life. See once you have the money, you have to have the power to feel complete. Now you and your people had some authorized hits that caused me some serious money. "But, I'm good. I'm giving you a real opportunity to work for me. You have big balls. This is your sister, right? "She is." "Well you have my sister as well. Pary'on facial expression said it all. "Your sister?" Yes Enrique's wife. "So what do you want from me? I need you to give me my sister and the kids. And you can have your sister, but you have to deliver her to me because Guadalupe and Cruz won't do it. She is only tied to Enrique. She has nothing to do with this, just like your sister. If anyone can do it you can do it. Make it happen. And he nudge Tania so she could leave with Pary'on. The women looked at Pary'on and Tania with very evil eyes. EL Tarpeta picked up the phone to call the driver. Let Mr. Pary'on and his sister out at the next full stop. EL Tarpeta just starred at them. The van stopped, then seconds later the side door opened. EL Tarpeta motioned with his hand pointing towards the exit. "I expect to see you within two days, or those guards you have around that mini mansion won't be enough to stop my rage. See you soon. Pary'on and Tania jumpes out into the beautiful night life of Miami. Pary'on grabbed Tania by the hand then moved across the busy traffic. Pary'on called to his help. "We cool." Come get us from the Veneto Hotel. "Approximately five minutes later Jorge came with a bulletprooof BMW 7 Series. Pary'on and Tania jumped inside. "You good!" Jorge asked. "For now. Go straight to my house. "Pary'on sat quietly thinking of a mastet plan. When they arrived ar the mini mansion, Pary'on had a game plan. He looked around as the gates slowly opened for Jorge to enter onto the premises. Pary'on got out first then walked to the side where Tania was seated. He opened the door and she got out. She hugged him tightly then she begins to cry as she buried her face into his chest. He patted her on her back then rubbed her. "It's okay. I was not gonna stop until I got you back. We safe now. Come on, the rest of the family is inside. "They walked across the massive driveway into the mansion. Once inside at the sight of Tania everyone cried, running up to her, hugging her and kissing her on the cheeks and forehead. "I'm sorry to break this up but we have to leave now! I don't feel safe for us here! We are boarding a private jet that will carry us to New York to safety! Let's Go! "And everyone started moving. "Twenty minutes later everyone was leaving to go to the airport landing strip. Pary'on led the way. As they stopped on the landing strip the doors of the plane was being open. The engine could have been heard as they begin to board the jet. The jet was now ready to go. Pary'on went to the pilot. "We are ready now. Thank you for meeting us on such rush time. Back to the compound. "Pary'on got on the phone to let Cruz know what his plan was. And they decided to talk more in person. As the hours past Pary'on looked at Marie interacting with her family. She and Tania held each other. Pary'on just was happy to be around his family again. His children were sleeping, then him and Marie locked eyes. He gave her a sexy sly smile and a nod. She walked up to her man. She kissed her man. "Thank you for bringing Tania home bae. I am sorry for neglecting us. "You don't have to explain. We are gonna make it. I am a different man now. The level I am at now is a level every man or woman in these streets wanna be. It's over, and I am serious. I promise we are gonna live better lives after this is over. We have two hundred and fifty million dollars. That's a quarter of a billion dollars. I'm done. I have the whole family back. I'll get back to our regular lives once this is over. The people I will introduce you to are loyal about family. So they will treat everyone here like they were around them their whole life. A good leader is one who carries the load of everyone on their shoulders. True leaders have a strong resolve and are tenacious in their pursuit.

When you have been inspired to accomplish a task, you go to bed with it on your mind and when you arise it's still there. If you quit before you are totally satisfied with your results, you will never fulfilled for wondering what could have been. So that's why I am going so hard for the family until it gets better. "And that's why I love you so much." And that's when Pary'on got evveryone's attention. "Family! Chek this out. I first want to apologize for what happen to my wonderful little sister. But this is a time we come together and stood ten toes. But, this is a moment for my kids and the woman in my life. There is absolutely no substitute for building Godly trust and loyalty in a relationships. You must touch the heart of your lover from this day forth. I am responsible for all the debts and obligations to this family and my future wife and kids. The way you were in our past relationship, when we first started this life journey, I should have run to the nearest jeweler to make you my wonderful wife. If I knew you as a kid, I would have run to the nearest machine with a pocket full of quarters trying to get you a nice ring out the bubble gum machine. I would of present you with that clear bubble top plastic with the ring inside with a big smile and a stuff animal. You are a very rare woman Marie. I really know you're worth it and I don;t want to lose out on the opportunity to have a loyal woman in my heart. Because I will not marry the woman that I can live with, but rhe only woman I can't live without. Will you marry me Marie? "Pary'on got on one knee, then Pary'on presented the 3.5 flawless normous circle with 2.24 carat of 12 baguette cut diamond set inside 18 carat yellow gold. Will you marry me Marie? "She stood there crying. The jet was silent. "Ye Baby! Yes. I thought you would never ask! "Pary'on placed the size 6 ring on her finger then got up and kissed his future wife. The rest of the jet ride was a bunch of celebrating, drinking the finest MOD selection champagne the product of France 1892 bottle. Once they landed it was multiple cars to take the family to Cruz compound. Once they made it there, Cruz, Guadalupe and Maria and Isabella was waiting. The driver stopped in front of Cruz's compound then Cruz opened the door for Pary'on. They were happy to see him in one piece. They hugged him dearly. Then Pary'on introduced Marie and his kids to them first, then came the rest of the family. Isabella walked off at the sight of Marie and her new ring on her finger. Love, jealousy and rage filled her up at one time at the sight of Pary'on happiness with another woman. Then Cruz talked up. "Well yall are Pary'on's family, yall are mine as well. Welcome to my compound. My chef will be asking everyone their special individual dishes for breakfast, lunch, and dinner. Do not be ashamed to eat what you like. Pary'on will tell you that none of my house is off limits except my bedroom. Please enjoy yourself its plenty to do here. And it's safe to drive any car as well or get the driver to take yall anywhere. All older family can live on the bottom layer of the house. Security is around twenty four seven, so feel safe. Make yourself at home. I was informed that yall will be going on a shopping spree tomorrow. Get what you need the bill will be on my friend here. "He patted Pary'on on the back. And laughter burst out. "But we as family will always be alright. Pary'on and I found a few compounds for sale at a small hefty price. I know you told me that you have to do it for your family. My real estate agent will be in contact when she gets back in the states. She is selling property in Australia. So she will go over everything with you, once she get back next week. So if you have to stay here until things clear up, please feel free to live your life. Come see me once you finish with your other family Pary'on. "I sure will." "Then everyone introduced each other as if it was a family reunion. Pary'on walked around the compound with Marie holding hands talking. Marie kept looking at her ring. "Do you like it baby? Are you krazy nigga! I love it! This is my happy ending! "Fosho." They did not see Isabella in the cut ice grilling Marie. She even went to the extreme as to have an infared beam on the back of Marie's head. But she knew Pary'on would kill her if he found out. And he was happy for many years. So she gave up for now. Now was not the time for her jealousy, so she took this as an "L". This was the first time Marie felt so complete. They were in a new love state. They made slow sweet love like it was the last time they would be with each other. Pary'on paid very close attention to Marie's body. He made her feel real special. She was back on cloud nine falling deeper in love with her future husband. They just held each other.

When they were finally finish their love session, Marie just rubbed her hand gently across Pary'on's body giving him small kisses as she laid on top of him as her head nested wonderfully on his chest. This was the night she dreamed about. She was with her happy ending. She fell asleep in minutes...The next morning Pary'on got up to play with his children. Marie slept in, but she got up to the loud laughter of her kids outside the open window. She sat up in the king size soft bed to stretch. She got up to look out the window to see Pary'on and the kids play wrestling on a big in ground trampoline. All she could do was smile. It was such a pretty sight. Then she got herself together then joine them outside. Isabella burned inside, as she sat on the fourth level patio smoking a blunt as stream of tears ran down her face. She was looking at a family that every woman dreamed of. Pary'on was every woman's dream husband. She knew that it would never be. She had to move on because the man she saved herself for would never cross that line ever again. He was too loyal to her family. She shook her head and coninued her blunt. Thirty minutes later Pary'on met with Cruz and Guadalupe. He explained his agreement with EL Tarpeta. They came to agreement terms. "After the exchange we will follow the GPS. We have the transmitter in his sister clothes. He might not take it straight there, but once you get to Flordia the chase will begin. We will at least know some of his whereabouts, so be careful Mr. Harmanous. I don't trust this. Why not his right-hand man as well, Guadalupe asked? Cruz chimed in. He want him dead. Being that he have been with us, he figured he already gave up to much information, trust me. The sister holds the info that can crush him. She was in the picture before Enrique. She knows everything. Let's do this. "And they got EL Tarpeta's sister and baby to board the jet. The door open to the spot where they are being held. Pary'on went to the females. "Come on with nme. Any funny shit and it's over. Let's go now! He held his gun in his hand. He escorted them to the car. The driver called on the phone. Wher to?" "The Jet!" Once they board the jet two hours later they ot off the landing strip to the car. They pulled up to the Club Creamy. Then Pary'on was approached by a small man that looked to be white of just a pale Cuban. I'm Pary'on, I need to speak to EL Tarpeta. "Follow me. Pary'on and the woman with her kids walked through the club following the short male. At the mention of her brother's name she becam very confident she and her children would be safe. They walked in front of Pary'on to a back room. "Sit here and someone will be with you Mr. Pary'on. Twenty minutes later they were escorted to the back club. A man standing 6'8, 305 pounds told Pary'on, "Sir your services are no longer needed. And the woman and kids were placed inside the car. The woman had a very confident look on her face as she starred at Pary'on. The car door slammed then he massive giant got inside on the opposite side of the stretch vehicle, then the vehicle pulled off. Then Pary'on felt weird. Another car pulled into the alley. Pary'on turned around to go back inside the club but the door was locked. He then begin to run as the car sped up towards him. As he ran he was almost to the dead end, he notices a door open and he ran inside. It was a lingerie shop. He ran past female models posing in all types of lacy beautiful lingerie. Shots rang out making him duck and dodge bullets. He ran out the store onto the sidewalk. Pary'on looked around then he notice some men that pointed at him once they saw him. He pulled out his Glock 40 pointing it at the men running towards him letting off shots. He used the opportunity to get to the car. He jumped inside then hit push start button holding on to his Glock 40 still. He drove off into traffic leaving the men behind him. It was on and popping now. Once he made it to the landing strip he cut the car off then his body relaxed. He waited till he got on the plane to call Guadalupe and Cruz. It was on tonight. It could not wait. He was going himself if he had too. He made it back to Cruz's spot. When he was waiting for the gate to open, he sat inside his new Porsche 718 Boxster as he was pullinf up to the main estate, he notice his family enjoying the Olympic size pool in the sun. His children rode banshee four wheelers. Everyone was doinf something. Marie was layinf out in lawn chairs in a bathing suit with her sister. They all enjoyed themselves. It was for sure everyone was getting use to this new lifestyle. Once Pary'on parked, his kids came running up to him, "DADDY!" Your back! "They both had on swimming attire. Werc yall in the pool? He said as he picked up his daughter. They both said, yea." in unison. Cruz and Guadalupe was playing golf. Pary'on got one of the golf carts and told his kids to go play because he had business to discuss. Once he was moving in the golf cart as he got closer he notice the men was smoking Cuban cigars. Once he walked up to he powerful men, his body language spoke a mile a second. "What happen m hermanos?" Guadalupe asked. "They tried to kill me after I made the drop. "Well we see you made it out alive.

We have the cordinates on EL Tarpeta Castle. Enrique was talking about. By the way he is dead. Isabella tortured him something serious till his heart gave out. Then she still cut him up with a baby chainsaw and fed his remains to the dogs. Pary'on eyes looks surprised. "The dogs eat humans?" Cruz shook his head yes, smiling. We have Akitas that are ruthless beasts" "Well I wanna move in on this nigga after Skeet funeral. Where is D-Block?" He went shopping for clothes. he went to get both of yall some tuxedos, plus he said he had to dress Skeet up. "They showed Pary'on EL Tarpeta's castle on a tablet. This is where we gonna send fifty soliders to infiltrate him. The transmitter points straight to his spot. She took the shoes off because they are no longer moving. The transmitter is still alive but its not active. So let's do this after Skeet funeral. "Then Pary'on told them what EL Tarpeta told him about Skeet. "Are you sure?" That's what EL Tarpeta told me." "Do you believe him?" I do. He said it trying to hurt me, but he added so much fuel to my fire. Nobody messes with my amily, Nobody! So I'm ready." "Then there is nothing else to be said. "And they went back to playing golf. Skeet funeral was packed. The fire marshals would have had a heart attack if they knew how many people was inside this one building. Pary'on had security for Mrs Pinkney and her family. Everyone was really mourning Skeet's death. That was the fastest traveling news ever. The whole city came out. It was a sad situation just like the Emanuel Nine. Everyone brought teddy bears, cards, flowers and T-shirts with Skeet's pictures on them. It was a very depressing time. Everyone always asked Pary'on if he was okay because they knew that Skeet was his best friend. Later that evening at the stroke of dark skies there was a firework show that lasted one hour. Skeet always said he wanted fireworks at his funeral and wedding. And he wanted a twenty-one gun salute. twenty-one close homeboys like brothers lined up together with their pistols then held theit hands in the sky pointing their pistols then they all let off a few founds for Skeet. Pary'on hated the comment EL Tarpeta said about Skeet switching sides. Pary'on would never believe an opp over his own personal judgement. Skeet knew everything about him and vice versa, so he refuses to believe any betrayal was involved. It was time for actions. As Pary'on tied up his loose ends at the party, he eased out rhe back with Rudy and D-Block. Tonight was the night. Everyone sat quietly as they board the jet. They all got some much needed rest on the flight. They got off the jet awaiting killera that was ready to infiltrate EL Tarpeta. They stop to the old mansion that Pary'on use to raid his arsenal. They all grabbed militaruy equipment from the storing arms and repertoire. Their plans was discuss over and over, so now it was all about actions. I did not take them long to get to EL Tarpeta castle. Pary'on had his night vision glasses on to pin point all the soliders on standby watch. Cruz and Guadalupe trained personnel ran up on some of the guards killing them smoothly. Then dragging their bodies to a safe location. Then Pary'on, Jorge, Rudy and D-Block and some highly trained men switch their clothes into the dead men attire. Now that was done, it was time for the next plan for them to get inside smoothly. Jorge led the way because his multi-language speaking was what they needed. He approached the side entrance and was let in just off the sight of his clothing. Then they all moved swiftly to the back door entrance to the massive main unit. EL Tarpeta was enjoying some of the greatest wine with a couple of friends. When he was interrupted. "Sir I think you should come here." El Tarpeta excused himself to he hallway. "Yes" There is movement inside the main house. It was reported by the top chef." Well let's go to the elevator to check on my sister and the children. I'm sure Enrique is long gone now. So all we have to worry about is her. At their arrival to the main house the chef ran up to El Tarpeta, "your sister is being quetioned by some of our soliders!" EL Tarpeta grabbed two men to go with him. He lead the way to his sister domain. Once they got off the elevator they saw two of his men outside the room. He began speaking in pig Latin.

The men spoke back not missing a beat. "Well let me in Now! And when they stopped to the side to let EL Tarpeta walk by that was when they snapped the men neck from behind leaving EL Tarpeta alone. Pary'on ran up on EL Tarpeta fast knocking him down as he punched him across his jaw.EL Tarpeta was taken by surprise. That's when Pary'on pulled his mask He now was at shock. Rudy begin using his I-phone X to record the events for Cruz and Guadalupe. "So you thought was untouchable?!" "Pary'on what are you doing here? I thought we had a pleasant exchange!" Pary'on slapped him. "Shut up bitch! You thought I would have been killed in that alley! Now you hae to answer to me, Guadalupe and his family! NO,NO,NO! See this is far bigger than I am! I just carry out orders! "For who!" Then he looked at his sister who was crying. "Who muthafucka! Pary'on screamed as he pointed his Glock 40 in his face. "Well Guadalupe's brother Carlos was young when he shot my father. And that really separated all of us because we all once were considered la familia! So my little brother Jesus is the king over the EL Diablo Cartel and my older brother Mario have power! So if you get me its greater force behind the scenes you will have to deal with! All your families will be killed. Carlos shot my father! That bullet was stuck in his head for a long time till it finally killed him! So the mark of death has been taking out until every ounce of Guadalupe's la familia blood is erased off the earth!" Pary'on walked up to EL Tarpeta sister then blew her brains out including her kids. Then he walked back up to EL Tarpeta, 'Well yours first bitch! My family ain't going no where! "Then he shot EL Tarpeta in his head. Then he stood over him and empited the clip in his lifeless body. They all left out running. Everyone in their way got shot or shot at until they made it back to the front kitchen where Jorge put a slice in the gas stove, Gas begin filing the kitchen area. Then D-Block begin drenching the house down with gasoline. The fire spread like wild flower all through the castle. Everyone began running as the big drapes caught a blaze. The massive rooms where there was a lot of furniture and steps that were wooden with a seventy foot long skinny rug was placed in the middle of the long steps caught fire. They made it out then all the personnel helpers around the castle ran out. It was pandemonium. They all made an exit to the van that was parked down the long driveway. Then it was a loud explosion. But the place was up in flames. They left Key West, Flordia to the jet to go back to New York. The trip back on the plane was dead silent one. This chapter of their lives were done. Pary'on could not wait to see the look on Guadalupe's face once he seen the recorded footage of tonight's event. Once the jet landed, Pary'on looked out the small window and saw four waiting cars. When he stood at the top of the entrance and exit of step, his family was waiting for him. Also Cruz, Guadalupe, Isabella and Mrs. Maria was waiting. they all smiled and clapped as Pary'on walked down the steps. Everyone on the plane had their family greet them. Their lives were soon to change. They put in a lot of work to live comfortable. They all celebrated until the wee hours in the morning. The next day Pary'on sat in the middle of the maze where Cruz, Guadalupe and Pary'on meet up for privacy.

Guadalupe and Cruz pulled up in one of the multiple golf carts used to get around the compound. The two greeted Pary'on. "Finally its over! Now I can go back home with my wife and daughter! "Guadalupe said happily patting Pary'on on his back. I'm glad to help out. You are my la familia. Then he passed Guadalupe the phone after he pressed play. And the action began. Both Cruz and Guadalupe bent over looking at he footage being displayed on front of the cell phone. Their eyes got big and locked in on the sight of EL Tarpeta. The mood changed once Guadalupe heard Mario name. "Guadalupe said. "It won't be long until the news of his brother, sister and niece's death will surface. Then he will start looking for answers. But his team won't make a move any time soon. That will give us time to prepare for rhe impact. It might be years before he gets the information unless he tries to get in contact with EL Tarpeta. Mario is all the way in South America living his life. He is on the run from America for killing a cop from Texas. He has been over there for tn years now. He won't step foot back over here. He is very ruthless, but it's been sometime since we last even heard anyone even talk about him. I ain't even worried. We about to head back home. If anybody want any problems we will get back together, if any of us need assistance. I want everyone to enjoy family life. I don't think we have anything to worry about." Then there was anioment of silence.

Pary'on got up to stretch. "Well fellas it was nice. I am going to enjoy my family life. I have a wedding to plan. I'll see you all there, right! "Cruz stuck his hand out and Pary'on shook it. "You can count on me being there. Don;t be a stranger either. And my real estate agent found a very nice place. I'm sure you would be very interested in Pary'on. Set up the meeting. I also have to purchase houses for Marie family members, four mansions should do, I'm going to enjoy life with all the money I got. Thank yall for everything. This wedding is gonna be epic.

She deserves it. Until next time, I love you both. I'll be in touch soon. "And Pary'on walked to the golf cart to go back to the main house to gather his family to leave. Cruz and Guadalupe watched as Pary'on left. Cruz looked at Guadalupe and said." "There goes one of the loyalist stand up men I've ever laid eyes on. He has a very bright future. Carlos always dealt outside the family, but this time I'm glad he did. We have another brother in our lives. Guadalupe I don't worry about him.He know how to handle himself. I'm sure we all will be under the same roof again soon.Hopefully we all wil be making a toast to the finer things in life. The holidays will be celebrated at Pary'on new house rather than his small island. They want one hundred million dollars. His family will love it, plus he will have his own personnel jet, "Sounds like he is set like us." "Like real Kings! Loyalty+Money=HAPPINESS!!!

THE END

LOVE PLUS LOYALTY

L+ L = REVENGE

COMING SOON

BY: DESHAWN B. HICKS

Printed in the United States
by Baker & Taylor Publisher Services